W9-DIZ-822

An Old-Fashioned Darling

By Charles Simmons: POWDERED EGGS

Charles Simmons

An Old-Fashioned Darling

Coward, McCann & Geoghegan, Inc.

 New York

To Peggy Brooks

An Old-Fashioned Darling

S OMETIMES Oliver thought he was in love with Long Island. Long Island was the most beautiful girl he had ever seen; and how many men, as he once put it to his friend and colleague Arf, have slept with the most beautiful girl they have ever seen?

Long Island had white skin with a touch of pink in the cheeks, green eyes, and black curly hair. Her legs were short; but she wore high heels, even when she walked naked around his apartment; and this not only disguised the fault, it brought back the bathing beauty contests he had watched on television in his adolescence. Her breasts were thin and pointed, like sweet potato halves; but the nipples were prominent and very erectile, so that Oliver felt an immediate sense of accomplishment when he began to play with them. She was not intelligent in the big-city sense of the word; nonetheless, Oliver could talk to her for hours on end and enjoy every minute of it.

She would tell him about her house and garden, her

two children and the affairs of other women in her sub-
urban community, about her new clothes and the car she
and her husband were buying; and often she discussed her
theory of "the sex people"—"I can recognize them,"
she would say. "They're *sexy*. They're *interested*. It's a
kind of underground. I know them, and they know me.
And most of them are married to *duds*." "You mean, like
Gus," Oliver would say. "Oh, God, yes," and she would
then describe Gus' latest failure in bed.

It all made Oliver feel that he was Long Island's real
husband, and Gus only an attendant. In fact, whenever he
visited them as a family friend, after a few drinks he would
think of the children as his children and drive back to
town at eighty miles an hour determined to take Long
Island, along with the kids, away from Gus. But the feeling would last only till the next day, when the practical
difficulties of such a step became all too clear to him.

Oliver's affair with Long Island had been going on for
two years. Although they met no more than once a week,
they spoke by phone almost every day. It worked this way.
They had an understanding that he would call at 9:15 in
the morning. If by 9:15 Gus hadn't left the house or for
some other reason Long Island couldn't talk, she would
take the phone off the hook and he would try the next
day. If he himself couldn't talk at length at 9:15 but
wanted to talk later, he would make the 9:15 call and ar-
range to phone from his office at, say, 2:00, when his boss
would not yet be back from lunch or her kids from school.

It was chancy for her to phone him, because long-dis-
tance calls were recorded on her bill. So if she had to

call—to warn him, perhaps, that her husband would be home at the time he was scheduled to make an afternoon call—she would use a pay phone. And, if he was not at his desk, their plan was for her not to leave her real name but say that Perdita was calling. Perdita was their danger signal. It meant that Oliver was not to call her until he got the all clear.

Only once had she used the signal. After staying at Brooklyn's place for the night, he had come in late to his office; and there on his desk was a note saying that Perdita had called. He waited seven days to hear from her. At exactly 9:15 on the seventh day he phoned her, and she told him that she had used the signal so that she would never have to talk to or see him again: the affair had made her feel like a whore. He in turn told her that he had been half crazy during the week, which was half true, and soon had her agreeing to come into the city for an exploratory lunch. They met at a restaurant within walking distance of his apartment and after the first drink sped there and to bed, where she made him promise that he would not abandon her if her husband ever found out.

The electric clock next to his bed said 9:13. Dressed for work, Oliver sat in the leather sling chair by the phone watching the second hand. At exactly 9:15 he picked up the receiver and dialed area code 516 but found he had forgotten the number itself. It had dropped from his mind like the name of an old friend about to be introduced at a party. He hurried to the hall closet, where he kept a filing cabinet that contained what he called his daybook, a record of sexual appointments and fulfillments, along with pertinent addresses and phone numbers. As it should be, the cabinet was locked, so he hurried back to the bedroom for the key. But when he opened the cabinet he remembered that he had left the daybook on the phone table under the Manhattan directory. By the time he dialed the number it was 9:17.

Long Island's phone rang at the other end and was picked up instantly, but no one spoke.

"Hi," he said tentatively.

"There's no Perdita here," Long Island said. "No, no Perdita," and she hung up.

Walking to his office, he wasn't upset. In fact, he found himself singing, "Yes, we have no Perditas, we have no Perditas today." What did trouble him was the fact that he had left the daybook on the phone table. Florida had used the phone the previous evening to talk to her husband. This meant that between engagement one and engagement two she had been alone with the daybook for half an hour. He tried to remember whether the second engagement had been different from the first. No, it was standard. And afterward, he had gone downstairs with her, put her into a cab; she blew a kiss through the rear window. All as usual. Anyway, even if Florida had examined the daybook, his lovemaking was coded in Greek initials. Thus Long Island was lambda iota, Brooklyn was beta, and Florida herself was phi.

His mind slipped to an old consideration. Shouldn't he refine his records? At present he kept only the date, the girl, and the number of times he had made love to her. Last night, for instance, was "8 17 phi 2." August 17, Florida, twice. Why not also the girl's orgasms? His and hers, which would have been "8 17 mu 2 phi 2," mu being the Greek initial for "me." Why not the hour of the day, too? The duration of the act, the fore- and after-play, the intensity of the climaxes, an evaluation of the satisfaction, the positions. If he had time during the day, he would work up symbols for the major positions. They might even make an amusing piece for the magazine.

As he sat down at his desk in the office, his phone rang. "Whom am I speaking to?" a strident female voice asked.

"Whom am *I'm* speaking toom?" he said. He was used to nuts calling the magazine.

"Is this Oliver Bacon?" The voice was familiar yet strange.

"Yes."

"This is Lillian Bauer, do you remember me?"

Remember? Lillian Bauer was Long Island. What was going on?

"Sweetie. . . ."

She talked over him. "I'm calling because something very serious has happened. I'm very upset. A woman phoned this morning and said the most terrible things. . . ."

"Hon. . . ."

"She said my phone is tapped and I'm being watched.

She accused me of seeing you. You have lots of girls, Oliver, and I'm sure they're crazy about you, but you can tell this one I'm going to the police. A friend of my husband's is an FBI agent, and I'll turn the whole matter over to him. If I wasn't afraid of upsetting Gus, I would have called him instead of you. I want to give that woman a chance, Oliver, because if she bothers me again I will see to it that she goes to jail."

"Lillian, I don't understand what she did."

"She said my phone is being tapped."

"You told me that."

"This woman accused me of having an affair with you. My God, I hardly know you. *I hardly know you.*"

"OK. What else did she say?"

"She said she had a photograph of me coming out of your house and that if I ever saw you again she would send it to Gus."

"No one could take a photograph of you coming out of my house without being seen, Lillian."

"*Seen!* I've never *been* to your house. I don't even know where you live. I haven't been to the city in six months. The last time. . . ."

"Where are you?"

"I was so distraught I had to get out of the house."

"Where *are* you?"

"At the shopping center."

"Well, what was all that crap about the phone being tapped? . . . Can you get into town for lunch? A sit-up lunch."

"Lunch? I can't have lunch with you. I hardly know

you. And what if I'm being followed? What if *your* phone is being tapped? I hardly know you."

"Lillian, I get the message. My phone isn't tapped."

"I'm not trying to get any *message* to you. I'm merely telling you that I'll go to the police if that insane woman calls again, and if you know who it is you can tell her so."

"Lillian, don't hang up." But she did.

Oliver went down to the lobby coffee shop and tried to figure out whether Long Island had been having a nervous breakdown by phone or had really received such a call. She surely was a guilt-ridden, nervous type; but there was never any evidence that she was actually cracked. In either case he would have to talk further with her. This meant calling her at home, which would be difficult, considering her suspicions. He went back to his desk and waited half an hour.

"Yes?" she said.

"Lillian, this is Oliver Bacon. I hope you're not too upset to talk to me, because I think this phone call business is very serious. Could you possibly come into the city and have lunch with me so that we could discuss it?"

"Lunch? Lunch? I hardly know you. . . ."

"OK. But we can talk now, can't we? You're not too upset to talk, are you? I understand about the phone and all, but it's very important that we talk. I mean, a crime has probably been committed."

"All right."

He sighed.

"What time did she call?"

"Twenty after eight."

"Oh. Now, tell me what she said. Try and use her words."

"She asked me if I was Lillian Bauer."

"Yes."

"Then she said she was calling as a friend, that she wanted to save me heartache."

"Did she use the word 'heartache'?"

"Then she said she knew we were having an affair, *claimed* we were having an affair. She said my phone was being tapped and there were recordings of our conversations, conversations I was supposed to have had with you."

"For Christ's sake!"

"Yes"—hysteria rose in her voice—"and she has a photograph of me leaving your house. . . ."

"Use her words!"

" 'I'll be forced to send the photograph to your husband. You'll be exposed before the entire community as an adulteress.' "

"Did she say 'adulteress'?"

"Yes, 'adulteress.' "

"That's some great word!"

"She said she was 'an angel of mercy.' "

"A *what?*"

"An angel of mercy."

"Oh, Jesus, I know who it is."

"Who is it?"

"It's a girl. But listen, your phone is not being tapped.

There's no photograph. This is all Southern fried bullshit. She had a Southern accent, didn't she?"

"She had an English accent."

"An *English* accent! What kind of English accent?"

"It sounded like a fake English accent."

"Fake how?"

"English on some words and not on others."

"Was it Southern at all? Think!"

"I don't know, Oliver. Oh, Oliver, I'm desperate. What will become of me?" She began to weep into the phone. "He'll kick me out in the street and take the children. Oliver, what will you do then? Will you kick me out in the street, too?"

"Honey, she's not going to tell Gus. And, even if she did, she has no proof. In the first place, phone-tapping is illegal. It costs thousands of dollars to have a phone tapped. And, as far as a photograph goes, she doesn't even own a camera. It was all bluff."

"Oliver, how did she know about me? You told her, didn't you?"

"I give you my word of honor, may I drop dead this moment on this spot, if I told her or anybody else about us."

"How did she learn then, Oliver? If you didn't tell her, she found out by herself and maybe she does have proof."

"I'll find out how she found out. The thing now is not to worry."

"Oliver, she's one of your girlfriends, isn't she?"

He didn't answer.

"She said you had lots of girls and a steady mistress and

she said you did dirty, perverted things with them. She's the steady mistress, isn't she?"

"What do you mean, 'dirty, perverted things'?"

"That's what she said."

"What do *you* say?"

"About what?"

"Do I do dirty, perverted things?"

"I don't know what you do."

"I mean, with you."

"I'm only telling you what she said."

"I want to know what you think."

"She *is* your mistress, isn't she?"

"Sweetie, we're not even sure who she is yet."

"*You're* sure."

"I'm *not* sure. The point is, not to worry, because nothing is going to happen."

"And if it does? . . . Oliver, if it does?"

"It's not going to."

"*If*, Oliver, I said *if*."

"I'll take care of it then."

"I'm not worried about *it*. I'm worried about *me*. Will you take care of *me? Me, me!*"

"*Yes, yes!*"

"You won't. I know you won't. You *won't*, you *won't*." And with a last sob she hung up.

Oliver's boss had a normal-size body under a thick neck and a large head. He laid his hand on Oliver's shoulder. "The tit bit, Ollie. Arf's here." From his tone Oliver knew that he had been standing nearby during the call. It wasn't that the staff shouldn't make personal calls from the office, but this was a very personal call, and hearing it somehow put the boss one up on Oliver. The boss enjoyed learning of people's weaknesses; they seemed to confirm his view of human nature. "Titty bitty, Ollie-dollie," he said and squeezed Oliver's shoulder. Oliver's stomach turned. The boss' fingernails were manicured; he cleaned them frequently with his letter opener and wore a gold signet ring on his right pinky. Commenting on these signs of vanity, Oliver once said to Arf, "Does he think he's *attractive* or something? If I were Mather, I'd go to the toilet and never come out."

Ernest Mather, whom everyone called Mother, was an unlikely editor for Quiff. By way of New England store-keepers he was descended from the Puritan clergyman Increase Mather and had no feeling whatever for the kind of thing Quiff dealt in. Some people claimed he originally got the job because the organization needed a respectable front for its one girlie magazine, others that Quiff was started reluctantly and Mather was thought just the man to keep it from the extremes of vulgarity. Actually, Quiff was very vulgar. But, whatever the reason, Quiff had done well under Mather's editorship. It was currently the second or third money-maker in the field.

Although it was August, the staff was working on the Christmas issue, which would come out in October. Mather, Oliver, and Arthur Arf, the corporate art director, assembled around a conference table in Mather's office. "Ollie, do you want to fill Arfie in?"

It was a rhetorical question. Every month when Arf, making his rounds of the organization's magazines, stopped at Quiff to lay it out, Mather would say, "Ollie, do you want to fill Arfie in?" and Oliver would straighten his clipboard, sigh, and begin describing the issue in progress.

"The thinking is this, Arfie. Our strongest piece is on an L.A. mail-order house that sells prosthetic sex organs—artificial vaginas and penises. They're supposed to be substitutes for surgery victims and the otherwise impaired. Actually, we figure most of them are used by fags masquerading in the dark as women, and the penises are just old-fashioned dildos with a new wrinkle." The plastic penises were realistically wrinkled, and Oliver repeated his pun. Arf made a little barking sound, and Mather smiled. "The other wrinkle is that the firm is run by a group of L.A. physicians, whom we're naming."

"Illustrations?" Arf said.

"That's the problem. They've put out this brochure," Oliver passed it to Arf, "with crummy line drawings, which we can't use. Now, if it wasn't the lead piece, we could leave it unillustrated or stick in a cartoon."

Arf turned through the pamphlet slowly, nodding, clicking his tongue, frowning. Oliver glanced at Mather and recognized once again the look of quiet satisfaction on Mather's face when someone in his presence was deep in sexual thought.

"Do you have any samples?" Arf asked.

Oliver shook his head.

"OK. Get one twat, one prick! We'll hook them up and photograph them on a bed. Zzzzz!"

"Terrific!" Oliver said.

Mather wiped his eyes and looked quickly from side to side.

"Terrific!" Oliver repeated and waited for Mather's assent.

"Nnnnn," Mather finally said.

"OK," Oliver continued. "Now the present schedule follows with the Norman Mailer interview on masturbation."

"Is he for or against?" Arf asked.

"Against," Oliver said.

"What's the matter with masturbation?"

"It causes cancer. Anyway, the girl who did the interview took a photographer and a kitten with her, and at just the right instant she tossed the kitten at Mailer's groin. This is a picture of him catching it, except that you can't see the kitten or Mailer's hands. How do you like it?"

"Jesus!" Arf said. "It really looks like he's taken a firm grip on himself. And that expression!"

"There was a question of libel," Oliver said, "but the lawyers cleared it. Do you buy the picture, Arfie?"

"Terrific," Arf said. "Who's the girl who did the interview?"

"Some little chick with steel tits. You wouldn't like

13

her. OK. Then the treasure hunt. Color of three guys and three girls looking for treasure on a Caribbean isle and finding it between one another's legs. The transparencies are set up."

"Any good?" Arf said.

"Usual," Oliver said.

"Where did you get it?" Arf said.

"Free-lance job. Right, Mother?"

Mather, alerted by Arf's sudden interest, answered carefully. "Yes, actually it *was* free-lance. But better than ordinary, I'd say, Ollie. Considerably better. In fact, I think it has genuine mood. You yourself, Ollie, said it reminded you of 'L'Avventura.' "

"What I was thinking of," Arf said, "was that it's a shame we don't initiate more of these pixshticks right here in the office. I might even be able to direct one myself."

Since Arf was in charge of art for all the organization's magazines, he worked directly for the publisher; and the more prudent editors of the individual magazines, like Mather, dealt with him cautiously. Anyone who had the publisher's ear had power. "Great idea, Arfie. Very great indeed. We'll get one up for you. Ollie, let's get cracking on a pixshtick for old Arfie."

"I was thinking," Arf said, "along the lines of an Easter egg hunt for the Easter issue. We could take a cast and crew up to the Berkshires for a weekend before the leaves turn."

"Oh, for Christ's sake," Oliver said. "How about diving for muffs in Tahiti?"

14

"Let's be serious, Ollie," Mather said. "The fact is we'd love you to do one for us, Arfie."

"OK, now that the spoils are divided," Oliver said, "shall we move on? Next is the December Whiff of Quiff. We've decided on a foldout-down rather than a fold-out-out. Mother favors a back shot of the April Quiff—who was very popular, I'll admit—but I'm for this Eskimo we turned up. . . ."

"Eskimo!" Arf said.

"Beautiful, a beautiful Eskimo girl."

"Come on!" Arf said.

"Seriously. She has funny little tits and everything, and kind of a biggish, flat-type ass. . . ."

"But she has a great nose, is that it?"

"Yes. Exactly. A great, great nose. . . . Oh, well, no-body sees it but me. Anyway, Mother agreed—since he and I disagree—that you should make the choice, Arfie. Then we have a piece called 'Will They Make It When They've Made It?' by an ex-priest who claims that when and if the Catholic clergy finally is allowed to put it in they won't be able to get it up. He argues that Rome's awareness of this fact is the main barrier. But we're absolutely stumped for a picture. Mother suggested commissioning a painting of a troubled middle-aged man."

"*What!*" Arf said.

"Now, wait a minute, Ollie! That suggestion was merely made in passing."

"I didn't know we had discarded it, Mother."

Arf felt the heat of office crossfire and retreated into

15

thought. Finally he said, "How about a color shot of a Roman collar and a black brassiere on a red rug?"

The three of them sat in silence, considering the idea. Oliver knew that Mather was waiting for his reaction, so he took his time. Then, just as the silence was about to become embarrassing and Mather would have to say something ambiguous, Oliver said, "Terrific, Arfie! What do you think, Mother?"

"Let's try it," Mather said. "If we don't like it we can always change it."

This was as affirmative as Mather got after letting Oliver make a decision, and sometimes Oliver wouldn't settle for it. He would say, "Well, you know, Mother, time is short; and, if we have any doubts, maybe we ought to keep thinking until we come up with something we all like wholeheartedly." When Oliver did this, an agonizing half hour followed while Mather worked his way through the discarded suggestions, slowly returning to the original idea. But today Oliver was eager to get through the meeting.

"Then the New Year calendar. The slides are set up. What we've done this year is deal entirely with three-quarter rear views. Peek-a-boos over shoulders, under arms, closing with an upside-down between the legs. For the last one I'm looking for a girl who doesn't show up like the Grand Canyon. Anyway, the whole thing's Mother's idea," Oliver said and gave Arf a covert pained look.

Oliver knew that the calendar idea was bad, but every

issue he withheld his own suggestions from one of the features and let Mather's proposal go through unchallenged and unimproved, always establishing that it was Mather's idea. "Why do you do that?" Arf once asked. "It's not that I want that creep's job," Oliver said. "It's just that I need a witness to his incompetence if he ever starts leaning on me." "Why would he do that?" "Who knows?" Oliver said, "but they don't call him Mother for nothing."

"Finally fiction, the geri, and the cover. Fiction is about a girl who likes to get licked but develops a poison pussy. It's a fantasy."

"Sounds good," Arf said.

"Na! It's all told in metaphor. It's called 'The Deadliest Flower,' and we have some very mucousy flowers to show you. The December geri is supposedly by an anonymous seventy-year-old millionaire who got rejuvenated by screwing in an airplane. He takes a girl up, puts on the automatic pilot, and bangs away like an eagle. The climax of the piece comes when he's in high gear and the plane slips out of automatic. Should he finish off the girl and chance crashing or jump out and pull the plane from its spin? You'll have to read it to find out. I wrote it myself. Now for the cover. . . ."

The tit bit proper followed, consisting of an examination of the available black-and-white photographs and a showing, after Mather's blinds were drawn, of the color transparencies. While Oliver worked the projector and delivered a running commentary, Arf sketched layouts and made notes on cropping. By the time the bit was

17

done, a dozen or so people from the other departments had wandered in to watch.

Near the end of the afternoon Oliver went to Arf's office, which for Arf's friends was a sort of sanctuary, maintained by donations from editorial loot. The lady in charge of Plants Aplenty, for instance, gave seedlings and cuttings, peat moss and plant food, figured clay pots, terraria and much advice. With her help Arf had grown an enormous avocado tree, which was currently in blossom, the only example of an indoor avocado blooming she had ever encountered. On the strength of the achievement, Arf asked her to go to bed with him; but she said, "Arf, you're such a fructifier it would be dangerous." The editor of Caveat Emptor, a consumer's magazine, donated a color TV set and a miniature refrigerator. The Food Fiesta editor, a genial young man with high color, periodically came through with tinned delicacies and expensive wines. The editor of Trip Tips turned over twelve garish paintings from the Haitian cultural consul and two zebraskin drums, gifts from a grateful hotel owner in Kenya. Arf was also on good terms with the organization's director of supply and thereby had some of the best office furniture in the building—mainly pieces that in redecorating had passed out of the suites of the corporate officers. However, one item he felt his office lacked he could not get—a couch. "Arfie," the director had explained, "I could have a rosewood and leather lounge down here in twenty minutes, but someone would catch you on it with a chick and you'd be out on your ass." Arf argued that as things stood he was doing it on the floor, and a couch would only make the peril more comfortable. But the director didn't believe him.

Now Arf listened to Oliver's troubles, sucking on an earpiece of his glasses like a professional counselor. When Oliver was done, Arf poured Remy Martin into two brandy glasses from the editor of Food Fiesta and said, "All right, so what do you want? Do you want to keep them both, drop them both, keep one—if so, which one?"

Oliver made a thinking sound.

"If you want to keep them both, do nothing! Look sad for a week, and Florida will think you've lost Long Island. Long Island will be back as soon as she's over the fright."

"Would you believe it, Arf, if I told you that Long Island is the most beautiful girl I've ever seen? How many men have slept with the most beautiful girl they've ever seen?"

"You asked me that already."

"Sometimes when we're screwing I pull back and look at her, and it overwhelms me. . . . On the other hand. . . ."

". . . she can be a pain in the ass."

"She'll read an article in Life, say, about venereal disease. Then the next time she comes to my place she'll find a pimple in my bush and accuse me of having syphilis."

"Literally?"

"Literally. She jumped out of bed, ran into the bath-

19

room, and wouldn't come out until I promised not to
touch her *in any way*."

"Was this before or after screwing?"

"Before."

"So what happened?"

"I promised. What could I do? She was getting hysterical: she'd miss her train, her husband would find out.
Anyway, she finally emerged, and there I was standing
with a tremendous erection. I asked her if she was going
to leave me like that."

"What did she say?"

She looked at me for a while—all the time ready to
run back to the bathroom—and then she went to the
kitchen and got a pair of rubber gloves."

"You're kidding."

"No."

"She grabbed you with the rubber gloves?"

"Yes."

"How was it?"

"It hurt like hell. But she's so beautiful! . . . Did I ever
tell you how I met her?"

"No."

"Well, not *met* her. Actually I'd known her for a few
years. I'd see her at parties. Well, at one party about two
years ago I was dancing with her and I happened to say,
'Why don't you let me take you away from all this?' I
didn't mean anything by it. I mean, 'all this' wasn't so
bad. But somehow it got to her. She looked me straight
in the eye with that special look, and my nose began to
run. . . ."

"Your nose began to run!"

"From emotion. My nose runs sometimes. Anyway, as I was about to leave, she gave me the look again and said, 'You don't ever call me.' I said, 'You mean, on the phone?' She said yes, and I said, 'OK, I'll call you,' and she said at quarter after nine Monday."

"And you were in."

"No. I had to call her every weekday for a month before she'd even come into the city for lunch."

"Then you were in."

"No. We had five or six lunches. *Then* I was in. Except when she'd get frightened. There was one period when she was afraid of getting pregnant, and even though she was on the pill she'd use her old diaphragm, I'd wear a rubber, and she'd douche afterward."

"That must have been a drag."

"But she's so beautiful! There have been times when I was absolutely sure I was in love with her. And there are times when I'm absolutely sure I'm not."

"How about now?"

"I don't know about now."

"What about Florida?"

"Florida is entirely different. She has no guilt whatever. Once Florida and I swam way out in the ocean and made love while her husband was sitting on the beach."

"How did you screw in the ocean?"

"It wasn't easy. In fact, some people saw us and sent a lifeguard out. They thought we were drowning. But Florida can be a pain in the ass, too."

"Like now."

"Exactly."

"So what do you want to do?"

"I don't know. Maybe I'll keep Long Island and dump Florida."

"It would be easier the other way around."

"I know, but Florida makes me uneasy. I think she's storing up grievances."

Arf shook his head. "A well-fucked woman has no grievances."

"Still, I think I better keep Long Island and dump Florida."

"Why?"

"Long Island's farther away. It's harder for her to get at me."

"That's rational. How about the other one?"

"Brooklyn? Brooklyn's not in the competition. She's single. No dodging husbands. No skulking around for quick matinees. I'll just hold her on the side."

"So you're all set. Just tell Florida to fuck off."

"I don't know, Arf. That's a dangerous woman. I mean, anyone who could make that phone call could also send me a poison apple or something."

"So what do you want?"

"I want proof that she made the call. Then I can get out indignant."

Arf thought a moment, then said, "Is she home now?"

"Probably. Why?"

"What's her number?"

"What are you going to do?"

"The number! The number!"

Oliver wrote it on Arf's memo pad.

Without a pause Arf picked up his phone and began dialing. "What's Florida's name?"

"Betty Lou Corn. Mrs. Betty Lou Corn."

"You're kid. . . . Hello, Mrs. Corn? . . . This is Arthur Arf, counselor-at-law. I'd like to talk with you. Do you have a moment? . . . No, now. . . . I'll tell you, I'll tell you. I represent a certain lady in Suffolk County. . . . Her name is immaterial." Arf made a face at Oliver, and Oliver wrote "Lillian Bauer" on the memo pad. "I'll tell you her name in due course. For the present let her be merely 'my client.' Now, Mrs. Corn, this morning my client received a phone call of a criminal nature. . . . I'm about to tell you what it has to do with you. Perhaps nothing, perhaps something. But I think we should talk, Mrs. Corn. A crime has been committed. Do you understand me? . . . Good! Now, Mrs. Corn, the person who made this call to my client accused my client, a married woman, of having an affair with a certain man. . . . Yes. My client was told that if she ever saw this man again she would be exposed before her family and the entire community as an adulteress. . . . I'll *tell* you what it has to do with you, Mrs. Corn. First of all, whoever made this call committed a prosecutable crime. I am a lawyer and I can tell you that a crime was committed this morning on the telephone. . . . Yes, I'm getting to that. Through certain connections I have with certain law enforcement agencies I was able to ascertain that the call was made from your phone." Arf held up crossed fingers for Oliver to see. "That, Mrs. Corn, is incontrovertible, computerized truth. From your phone at exactly . . . just let me check." Oliver mouthed the words "eighty twenty." "At exactly eight twenty, Mrs. Corn. Now, we could do a number of things with this information. We could feed it back to said law enforcement agency as a complaint. Or we could call up your husband at his office." Arf made a questioning expression at Oliver, and Oliver nodded. "Yes, at his office. We would, of course, tell him the whole story and ask him where *he* was at eight twenty this morning—men have been known to imitate women's voices. At any rate, we would ask him where he thought *you* were at eight twenty this morning. Now, Mrs. Corn, let me say here and now that frankly I don't know whether you made the call or not. All I know is that it was made on your phone. The crime of blackmail has been committed, and all I ask is that you see to it that it is not committed again on your phone. Can I have that assurance, Mrs. Corn?" As Arf listened to her reply he held up his free hand, thumb and index finger touching in the circle of success. "That's *wonderful*, Mrs. Corn, *wonderful*. And may I say that you are a lady of perception and discretion, and also that you have a charming drawl. Here's to you, Mrs. Corn!" He hung up.

"You genius you!"

"Wait! It's one thing for *me* to know about it, but she's got to admit it to *you*."

"Will she?"

"You said she's coming over tonight? When she does, look grave! Let her in and look grave! Whatever she says, whatever she does, you say nothing! Watch her! Wherever she moves in the room, watch her! Gravely! She'll confess."

"Why?"

"She'll assume that I called Long Island and Long Island called you."

"You're right, Arfie."

That evening Florida arrived "squeaky clean," as she put it, from her weekly swim at the YM&WHA. She had not learned to swim as a child, having been brought up in the Florida interior far from lake or river; but now that she and her husband were thinking of buying a summer home on Cape Cod she had signed up at the Y for lessons. In a year and a half she had been graduated from nonfloater to junior lifeguard. She once explained her progress to Oliver: "It's all because Ah'm swimmin' to get to *you*. When Ah'm strokin' up and down that pool, Ah think to mahself, 'He's right there waitin' at the divin' board,' or 'He's right there waitin' in the dressin' room,' or 'He's right there in the lobby,' an Ah just swim along like a hungry alligator. Yum, yum, yum!"

This evening her squeaky-clean routine began as usual. Standing in the doorway, she said, "Don't *touch* me, Oliver! Ah *reek* of chlorine. Don't come *ne*-ah me!" Ordinarily he would have made mock-ape sounds, taken her into his arms—actually she smelled of lemon perfume after swimming—and covered her with kisses. But tonight when she said, "Keep your *distance*, Oliver, Ah'm *vir-*

ginal. For sixty minutes chlorine's been washin' in and out of all mah *ori*fices. Swish-swash, Oliver"—when she said it this evening, he moved back.

For a few seconds she stood silent in the doorway, then swept in, dropping her drawstring bag on the floor. "Oliver, Ah know that dirty-minded people have an aversion to cleanliness, so ah'm goin' to admit that mah left ear stayed *above* water. You can come over and give it a *kiss*. She turned her left side to Oliver, but he retreated farther into the living room and stood in front of the couch.

"Are you rejecting mah left *ear*, Oliver? It may never for*give* you. You may want to whisper sweet nothings into it some day, and it won't tell me what you *said*, Oliver."

Oliver remained silent.

"Oliver, what's the matter?"

Whenever she dropped her naughty-Southern manner for her throaty, straight self, as she did to indicate the beginning of her sexual arousal and as she did now, he was moved. He almost broke his silence.

But she went on. "Oliver, if you don't want me here, all you have to do is say so. . . . Are you going to take out one of your foul moods on me, Oliver? . . . Why is it every time we have a thing I have to dive in and make the rescue? . . . And I don't even know who's drowning, Oliver. . . . You're standing there like a fool, Oliver. . . . There was an idiot in front of the drugstore in my town who looked just like you do now, and I'd say, 'Hello, Francis, how is the world treating you?' and he'd do just what you're doing—nothing. . . . Oliver, I don't know whether to laugh or cry. . . . Remember that time you wanted to sleep under the bed because your little thing wouldn't work? Do you know what most women would have done? Gotten dressed and gone home. But I got under there with you, didn't I? And made it work out just fine, didn't I, Oliver? . . ." They stood facing and watching one another, perhaps for a minute. "Oliver, did someone tell you about something today? . . . I assume someone told you about a phone call. . . . Oliver, will you answer me? . . . Oliver, if I leave this apartment now, you will never see me again, do you understand? . . . Do you want to talk about it or not? Because if you do, you'll have to tell me who told you and what he said. . . ." There was another period of silence. "Oliver, I only did it because I love you. Do you understand what that means? Do you understand the meaning of the word? 'Love!' " and she rushed toward him, head lowered, sobbing.

He held her off by her shoulders and guided her into a sitting position on the couch. Then he took a chair opposite, still observing her silently and gravely.

"It was because I love you, Oliver. I was trying to protect what we *had,* the little we *had.* God knows, it wasn't much, Oliver, but it was *ours.* No. I don't mean that. It was *mine.* Or was it, Oliver? Was it ever mine, that little thing? That little thing we had together? Or was it no one's? Rented out like a rent-a-car. Oh, and, my God, I was angry! How do you think it felt, seeing my most intimate, most personal acts recorded in a book like the weather? And the unkindest cut of all, Oliver, was that you wanted me to see it, didn't you?" Again he almost protested but stopped himself. "Left there in that nasty little book for me to see. Watch out! Don't get serious! There are others! You're only one of a number! In fact, I am a number, aren't I, Oliver? How much more manly it would have been of you, Oliver, to have told me your feelings face to face! And that petty trick to make me think you didn't want me to know! Lambda iota, Oliver! Oliver, I was pledged to Lambda Iota Kappa, you knew that. Did you pick your little Lillian with that in mind, like some kind of Joycean joke?"

Again he almost interrupted to correct her.

"Why, Oliver, you even provided me with Lambda Iota's phone number. Don't deny you didn't want me to call her! And who is Beta, Oliver? Not *this* Betty Lou, I could tell from the dates. Oh, Oliver, don't I deserve better? That I should be a phi! Is that all I am to you, a good f?"

She continued talking for thirty minutes, her mood and manner shifting from contrition to righteousness to anger and back again. At one angry point she rose and picked up her drawstring bag, as if to leave. It was intended only as a gesture in a succession of gestures that would end in reconciliation and bed; but Oliver, with artful timing, caught her elbow, ushered her to the door and out into the hall. Then, immediately and audibly he threw the double lock, attached the safety chain, poured himself a drink, and settled down in front of a soundless television picture to think.

After a while the silent television palled and he put

a pile of records on the phonograph to accompany it. As each record changed he poured himself another drink. A little after 2 A.M. his telephone rang. He had been half expecting it: Florida calling to patch things up and maybe if her husband was out of town to invite him over for the rest of the night, and he was half inclined to accept the proposal.

Instead it was Long Island, talking in hushed, hysterical tones. "Oliver, I've done something awful. I can't believe what I've done. How could I have made such a mistake? I've ruined my life, I've ruined Gus' life, I've ruined the children's life, *I've told him!*"

"What?"

"I told him."

"You told him! *Everything?*"

"Everything."

"Where are you?"

"I'm home. He rushed out of the house and took the car. Oliver, I'm so frightened!"

"Does he know where I live?"

"You're in the phone book, Oliver."

"Oh, Jesus! Well, don't panic, sweetie!"

"How could I have done such a thing, Oliver?"

"I don't know, sweetie. How could you?"

"I thought she'd tell him, Oliver. I thought she'd tell him and it would go all the worse for me."

"Sweetie, she wouldn't have told him. All she wanted was to break it up between you and me. She doesn't care about you."

"Oh, Oliver, somewhere in my head I knew that. How

could I have been so stupid? Oliver, he was so angry! He looks like my father when he's angry. I thought he was going to kill me."

"What did he say?"

"That's the terrible thing, Oliver. He didn't say anything. I just went on talking."

"Oh, for Christ's sake!" Oliver said, remembering how well his own silence had just worked on Florida. "How much did you tell him? Did you tell him how often and everything?"

"I toned that down a little."

"What exactly did you tell him about how often?"

"I told him we had been together three times."

"Three times!"

"She couldn't possibly prove more than three times, Oliver."

"Sweetie, she couldn't prove once. She couldn't prove we held hands. . . . All right, so what about the three times? When were the three times supposed to have happened?"

"Over a two-year period."

"Three times, over a two-year period!"

"You don't understand, Oliver. That struck Gus as just right. I could tell when I said it."

"What about the love thing? Was it supposed to be love, or just sex, or what?"

"I said you were crazy in love with me and you threatened to commit suicide if I didn't come into the city and have lunch with you."

"Lunch!"

"Yes, and I did, and after a few drinks one thing led to another, and then the other two times you also threatened to commit suicide."

"That makes you sort of a nurse."

"Yes. But still he was absolutely furious. I've never seen him so furious. . . . Oliver, I hear something. Oliver, I'm frightened." There was a silence for about thirty seconds, then, "It was the cat. I thought I heard him in the driveway."

"Sweetie, you weren't supposed to be in love with me at all, is that it? You sort of just felt sorry for me? Suppose I called Gus up and told him that every week you used to leave here with a sore twat?"

"Oliver!"

"I don't know, sweetie," he said wearily, the booze gathering up on him. "Good night, sweetie!" he said and put the phone down.

He poured himself still another drink and took it into the bedroom but fell asleep before drinking it.

"My plan now," Oliver said to Arf, after reporting Florida's confession to him and Long Island's confession to her husband, "is to cut down. I mean, I have to double-lock my door to make sure Gus dosen't bust in and bash me."

"Have you heard from Long Island again?"

"Not a word."

"And Florida?"

"She phoned. She wants to talk. I told her I was very confused and I had to settle some important questions in my life before I could talk."

"What did she say?"

"She wants me to go to her psychiatrist. Actually I *am* confused a little. I mean, what have I been banging all these dames for?"

"For fun."

"I guess so. Anyway, my plan now is to go with Brooklyn more or less exclusively. She's not married, so I don't have to meet her on the sly or anything, and it's someone I can take to parties and dinners and that sort of thing."

"Are you going to marry her?"

"Not unless I love her."

"Do you love her?"

"I don't think so."

"She'll think you're going to marry her if you start taking her everywhere."

"Not Brooklyn."

"They're all the same."

"Maybe, but *I'm* different."

"Baby, you're more like everybody than anybody I know."

Brooklyn was fine except when she was drunk; then she talked about death.

The first night he met her, one year before, they went to her apartment in Brooklyn Heights, got drunk, and she told him in detail about the deaths of her three friends, two aunts, and Adlai Stevenson. It seemed that death was always on her mind, but particularly in August; all these people had died in Augusts.

On that first night she had stripped to her panties and bra because the air conditioner was broken. Short, with a full figure, she marched up and down the living room, holding herself like a drum majorette to reinforce what she was saying. "And I will die in August, too. Maybe not this August, but some August. When all the rest are gone, my August will come around at last. I can feel death under the couch, my friend." He looked where she pointed, and it did seem ominous there. "It hangs on the rug like a green mold. But don't be afraid! You're safe. My grandfather died of mustard gas in August. No August passes, my friend, except *this* one. What would you say if I told you I haven't been to bed with a man for a year? What would you say if I told you that last August I made a promise not to sleep with anyone until this August was over? And in exchange no one would die? What would you say, my friend?"

"What is this, August twenty-what?"

"Twenty-second, my friend. Three o'clock in the morning of the twenty-second of August."

"And no one has died yet?"

"And no one will, my friend. What would you say to that?"

"I'd say that was OK. I mean, if you believe in it, as

you obviously do—that, after all, is the important thing. A lot of people might not think it makes any difference what you do or don't do by yourself here. But if you believe in it, that's the crucial thing. Absolutely crucial," he said and clicked his tongue.

"You don't believe in it, do you?" she said, leaning toward him.

"I don't really have an opinion one way or the other about the final validity of the thing. My feeling is, simply, if you feel it's right you certainly should follow your feeling, because if you didn't and then something happened you'd never forgive yourself."

She fell on her knees in front of him—he was sitting on a straight-backed chair—and squeezed her waist between his legs. "Will you come and sleep with me when August is over, my friend?"

"Yes, I certainly will. I'd like to very much. And may I ask you something, too?"

"Yes."

"Will you please not call me your friend?"

"I will never, never call you my friend again," and she mashed her mouth against his.

Actually they didn't wait for the end of August but went to bed that night. The next day the local Congressman died. He was a great favorite of Brooklyn's, and she blamed herself for his death. That had been a year ago.

"There's something different about you now," Brooklyn said.

"You mean because I'm staying the whole weekend?"

"No, because you look philosophical. You don't seem harried."

"I always thought I was a pretty calm-type person."

"Tonight is the most relaxed I've ever seen you."

"That's because tomorow's Saturday and I don't have to rush around and see anybody. What'll we do tomorrow?"

"We could stay in bed," Brooklyn said.

"Hey, we could."

"Do you want to?"

"Yeah," he said. "Let's stay up late tonight and not get up till late tomorrow. We'll get up about six and go over to one of those Arab restaurants for dinner and then stay up late again and then hit the sack early Sunday night and get up early Monday morning and have a big breakfast. What do you say?"

They were both naked. She had her head in his lap. Smiling, with her eyes closed, she turned it back and forth.

"Easy!" he said, but it was too late, and they made love on the couch.

The television movies were so bad they put on the radio and opened a bottle of bourbon. He drank more quickly than she, because he expected her to tell her death stories. Instead she talked about how always, secretly, she had wanted to be an aviatrix. He said it was strange she had never mentioned that before. She explained that it was a very deep desire, which she had repressed for fear of never fulfilling it. He said there was no reason in the world why she couldn't become an aviatrix and a damned good one. Her coordination was excellent; her endurance superior; and she had courage, too. Would she take him up for rides when she became an aviatrix? "Of course," she said. Could they put the plane on automatic and screw in the air? "You bet," she said and bit him on the nipple.

They made love again that night, in bed, and still again the next morning. While lying there afterward he asked her what kind of protection she used now. "I haven't seen you juggling with the diaphragm lately."

"I hate those things. I hate the *idea* of those things. I'm not even going to wear glasses."

"You don't need glasses, do you?"

"No, but when I do I'll have a big piece of glass ground to the formula and mounted over a reading table. The glasses wouldn't be on me, they'd be on the book, where they belong."

"So what are you using, the pill?"

"Ung!" she said and sat up convulsively. "Cramp!" She kicked the covers off and held out her right foot. The second toe stood straight, even bent a bit backward. She got out of bed onto her left foot and right heel, and, making sounds of distress, walked around the room. "It's going." She walked more. "It's going," she said and went into the living room. He heard the bathroom door close and fell asleep.

Later she sat down on the edge of the bed dressed in blouse and slacks. "Breakfast," she said, reaching under the bedclothes to tug his penis. He tucked it between his legs, then opened his eyes. "You're all dressed. We were going to spend the day in bed."

"I can get undressed again. Come have breakfast!"

She had fixed fried and basted eggs on pancakes inside a ring of bacon, along with orange juice and coffee. To compensate for his nakedness he sat particularly straight and ate with delicacy. After cigarettes he said again, "I thought we were going to spend the day in bed."

"Ah, the baby is still sleepy-poo," she said and, taking him by the arm, led him back to the bedroom. Gently she pushed him onto the pillow and covered him up. He dreamed of being grown and yet in a baby carriage. It was a cold, sunny day in early winter. He was wrapped against the weather. He complained to his nurse or mother that he could not move. Mistaking his complaint, she tried to feed him. He remembered that he had once liked the taste of milk from a bottle, but now it was thick and too sweet. He pushed the nipple from his mouth with his tongue, and she returned it. Finally he fell asleep in his dream and awoke in his dream to find himself still in the carriage, hurtling downhill. All he could see was the sky. The white clouds looked so benign against the blue that for a time he did not believe he could be hurt, particularly if he held himself rigid. But the carriage went faster and faster. He was about to give himself up to the inevitability of disaster when he awoke, gasping for breath. He tried to throw off the bedclothes, but his arm was asleep. He thought he heard Brooklyn in the living room. "Sweetie, are you there? *Sweetie!*"

She wasn't, and by the time she came home he was shaving. She poked her head into the bathroom, flushed and damp from the heat outdoors. "Hi there, sleepy-poo!"

"Sweetie, you didn't tell me what you use."

"For what?"

"Contraception."

"What's the big thing about contraception?"

"Tell me!"

She withdrew from the doorway and called back, "Maybe I'm sterile."

He put down his razor and hurried to the kitchen, where she was unpacking groceries. "What do you use?"

"Nothing."

"Nothing!"

"Nothing."

"How long has this been going on?"

"Two weeks."

"Are you crazy?"

"Oliver, all my life I've been on the side of death, and now I'm on the side of life."

"Are you pregnant?"

"Not that I know of."

"When was your last period?"

She looked down—he could not tell whether in anger or reserve.

He took her by the upper arm and gave it a small, firm, threatening shake. "When?"

"Two weeks ago."

"Two weeks ago! We were dead center last night."

"Oliver, this is entirely my affair. You won't know a thing about it."

"I already know about it."

"I'd bring up the child myself. I'd move to Switzerland."

"Suppose it's a boy. It'll be a fag."

"I have plenty of men friends who can offer it male companionship."

"In Switzerland? You've never been to Switzerland. What are you *talk*ing about?"

Brooklyn looked down again, into the shopping bag, and resumed unpacking. Oliver went to the bathroom to think and got into the bath he had drawn. He stayed there so long he had to reheat the water twice. Finally Brooklyn came to the door and asked him if he still wanted to go out to dinner. He had decided that the best strategy was to keep his head, so he said yes.

After dinner, at his suggestion, they went to a revival of "A Place in the Sun." Not until Montgomery Clift lets his pregnant girlfriend, Shelley Winters, drown did he realize that Brooklyn might think he had chosen the movie for the message. He turned to tell her he hadn't; but her eyes were already closed, tears coming out. "Let's go," he said and gave her a dig in the shoulder with his thumb. They took a taxi home in silence. As they drove into her block she said, "You can keep the cab and go if you want." He said, "Do you want me to?" She hesitated and said, "No."

Upstairs he settled in front of the television; his appetite for a movie had been aroused and not satisfied. There was a Canadian documentary about animal diseases and a science-fiction film with Virginia Bruce. He picked the science-fiction film. Halfway through it Brooklyn said she was going to bed—he could stay up if he wanted. He said he would join her in a little while. After the science-fiction film he watched a remake of "The Scarlet Pimpernel." Halfway through that, he went quietly into the bedroom. Brooklyn was asleep. He went to the kitchen, closed the door, and phoned Arf.

"Did I wake you up?"

"Yeah."

"Can you talk?"

"Sure."

"I mean, are you alone?"

"Even if I wasn't, I could talk. We go with different breeds of broad, Oliver."

"You said they were all the same."

"Not if you train them right."

"I'm over at Brooklyn's."

"Yeah?"

"I've been here since yesterday."

"Yeah?"

"This afternoon, just in passing, I asked her what she was using for protection. Do you know what she said? 'Nothing.'"

"Protection for what?"

"Birth control."

"Nothing!"

"Nothing. My ass fell off."

"Is she pregnant?"

"She says no."

"OK. She says she's not pregnant. Take her word for

it! Go home! It's been swell to know you, a wonderful
relationship; but now you have to go home. Is she asleep?"
   "Yes."
   "Leave her a note! Go now!"
   "Her period was two weeks ago."
   "She told you that?"
   "I asked her."
   "You banged her tonight?"
   "Last night and this morning."
   "OK. Let me think!"
Oliver put the phone down and went to the bedroom.
Brooklyn was still asleep.
   "Arf?"
   "I'm still thinking."
   "Take your time!"
After another minute Arf said, "OK. Now, either she's
being honest with you or she isn't, right?"
   "Right."
   "If she's being honest, she's not pregnant *as far as she
knows.* Right?"
   "Right."
   "On the other hand, if she's not being honest, there
are all sorts of possibilities. She may already be pregnant
and was planning to tell you, and you opened the box
with your question about contraception, so she decided
to begin by breaking it to you gently. Also, if she *is*
pregnant and told you she *was* using protection it would
be all the harder to get through to you eventually that
she was pregnant. You follow me?"
   "Sort of."

"OK. Now, if she *is* pregnant and knows it, she wasn't made pregnant last night. She's been pregnant for at least a month. Were you banging her last month?"

"Off and on."

"Be more exact!"

"Arf, I've been banging her for a year, every week or so."

"And this was the first time the protection thing occurred to you?"

"Of course not! It's just that recently I haven't noticed her using anything."

"OK. Have there been other guys?"

"She wasn't a virgin when I met her, if that's what you mean."

"Recently, recently!"

"I don't know."

"How come she's not married?"

"Maybe because she's been going with me. I don't know, Arf."

"All right, let me ask you something. Do you think she'd like to marry you?"

"I don't know."

"Don't be modest! Say it!"

"I don't *know*."

"Well, I think she would."

"Maybe she would."

"Don't kid yourself! Every woman wants to get married, and this one may be desperate, *desperate*."

"She's desperate to have a child, I know that."

"Your child or any child?"

"Arf, I don't *know*. This is all getting very abstract. I just want to know what to do."

"OK. Now, either she's telling you the truth as she knows it or she's not, right?"

"We've been through that, Arf."

"I know we have. What I'm getting at is that in either case you do the same thing."

"Which is what?"

"*Stick close and no fucking!* If she *is* pregnant, you want to know as much about it as possible—the when, where, why, and especially the who. If she's *not,* you also want to know. You wouldn't like her to *say* she's pregnant when she's not, would you?"

"She wouldn't do that."

"Look, baby, I don't know Brooklyn, and maybe you do; but women have been known to say they were pregnant when they weren't."

"I still don't think she'd do it."

"Great! Then you have nothing to worry about."

"Except if she's pregnant."

"Oh, my God! Do you realize that if she's pregnant by you as of last night she tricked you into it, do you realize that?"

"Yes, in a way."

"And if she could trick you by doing it she could trick you by saying it. Come on, baby, use your noodle!"

"I guess so."

"OK. Stick close! At the first trickle, you're off the hook. You don't want to miss the first trickle, right?"

"No."

"OK. And no fucking! In the first place she may have the two weeks wrong. Two weeks may be next Tuesday afternoon. Or maybe she remembers right and her ovaries forget. Or maybe her unconscious is giving your unconscious a chance to knock her up."

"What?"

"I mean, maybe your unconscious would really like to marry her, but your conscious won't let you. So this little episode gives your unconscious a chance to work your conscious over. Her unconscious, in fact, may know this and have started the whole thing. Or maybe her conscious knows it and is conspiring with your unconscious to force your conscious."

"I lost you."

"The point is, no fucking!"

"No fucking."

"And stick close!"

"Stick close."

The next two weeks were full of contradictions for Oliver. In principle he could not help but be sympathetic with Brooklyn. After all, he was strongly on the side of life himself, and although there were no further discussions of the subject with her he thought he might let nature take its course. If the worst happened he would support the child. He would do this without even being sure he was the father. A child is a child, a child is a human being. Does it really matter who feeds it? He reckoned the amounts it would cost per week and per year and deducted them from his weekly and yearly salaries. Sometimes the remainders seemed adequate to live on, sometimes not. When they weren't, he considered going to Mather and asking for a raise to the exact amount of the support. Thus Quiff would be paying for the child. This was not an entirely satisfactory solution, however, since future raises would thereby be consumed.

There were even moments when he considered accepting his fate completely, just as millions of men had, from time immemorial, done before him. Is there a better reason for marrying than to provide a home for a child? As to Brooklyn—she had good bones, she would last. If she didn't get fat. There were suspicious bumps around the thighs. He imagined cuddling a fat Brooklyn. As for drinking, it might disappear with maternal responsibilities. If not, of course, the death stories could make life pretty difficult. All told, after a thorough evaluation of the pros and cons, he decided he would rather be dead. "Dead!"

"What?" Brooklyn said from the couch.

"Nothing, sweetie. I was just talking back to the television."

This was the third weekend in a row that he had spent at Brooklyn's, and certain defects of the apartment had begun to bother him. The phonograph was monaural; there was no window in the kitchen; many ancient foods crowded the refrigerator—they even communicated their odors to the beer cans so that he had to pour his beer into a glass; the living room rug shed; plus other, lesser annoyances, hardly worth mentioning, except that they were all gathering to make him uncomfortable. Still, he wanted to follow Arf's advice and stick close.

Starting Friday evening of the third weekend, he searched surreptitiously for signs of menses. There were no used napkins in the waste disposal places and no new ones at the ready so far as he could see. A girl once told him that her stomach swelled during menses. Brooklyn wore slacks at home, and there was no apparent swelling. Nor did she show crankiness or fatigue. She seemed in a great mood.

As for the no fucking, it was less difficult than he had expected. He used the excuse that he had a touch of prostatitis, which he described as "an old complaint," even though he wasn't sure what prostatitis was. To this, Brooklyn said that she was pleased he "wanted to be with her anyway."

Saturday evening, watching television, he made a plan. When they went to bed he would tell her that his prostatitis had improved. If she was menstruating, this would force her to admit it. If she pleaded a headache or some such dodge, he would wait till she was asleep and make an investigation. Even Tampaxes have little strings hanging out.

After he got into bed, she spent an inordinate time in the bathroom. Was this good or bad? What *was* good or bad? His heart began to beat fast; he couldn't control his breathing. When she finally appeared, she shone like an apple. She seemed to know something was up. The instant she slipped in beside him he said, "My prostatitis

is getting better, sweetie." "Ooo!" she said, and they
knew each other in record time. They knew each other
twice again during the night. When he woke in the morning, instead of feeling open and easy, he was crowded by
bad thoughts.

He left her sleeping and went to the bathroom to pee
and brood. There he found, ringing his member, the
marks of menses. His genital had never looked so good
to him. Silently, swiftly, without shaving or showering,
he dressed; and only a sudden qualm brought him back
from the hall door to the kitchen table, where he left a
note. It looked like a little poem.

> Trouble back.
> Very painful.
> Gone to doctor.
> Let you know.

Oliver took a cab home from Brooklyn Heights,
picked up the Times at his doorstep, showered and got
into bed. He looked through the main section. As usual
on Sundays, there was no real news. The phone rang. He
counted eleven rings. He reached for the sports section;
it rang again. When it stopped he got up and took the
receiver off the hook. After the travel and business sec-
tions he put a pillow over the receiver and went back to
bed. He checked the editorial employment ads; but all
the jobs that paid more than his were for specialists—
med ed, sci ed, bus ed. No cnt ed, he thought; and he

began to consider a short feature for the magazine on
obscene want ads. In the middle of the arts and leisure
section he realized that he was still listening to the buzz,
so he got up and put the receiver back on the hook. Immediately the phone rang. When it stopped he took the
receiver off again and carried the paper into the living
room. He flicked through the real estate section and read
an article in the magazine section on electoral college
reform. There seemed to be a section missing. As he tried
to figure out which one, he fell asleep.

He woke in the dark to the sound of a phone ringing
in his dream. After a quick supper he watched television
till midnight and went to bed expecting sleeplessness,
but he fell right off and slept through till Monday morning. He replaced the phone just before he left the apartment. As he started down the stairs he heard it ring.

At ten o'clock in his office Brooklyn called from her
office to ask how his prostatitis was.

"So-so, sweetie."

"Your phone was busy all day yesterday and all night,
too."

"I took it off the hook. The doctor gave me a pretty
powerful drug."

"I had a picture of you lying unconscious on the floor."

"I was only asleep."

"Oliver."

"Yes."

"I thought you were going to die."

"It's not that serious, sweetie."

"I called my doctor about it last night."

"About what?"

"Prostatitis."

"What did he say?"

"He never heard of anyone having it at thirty."

"My doctor said it was pretty rare, too."

"Oliver."

"Yes, sweetie."

"You went away because of what happened, didn't you?"

"What happened?"

"I shouldn't have let you."

"Let me what?"

"Make love to me when I was sick."

"Oh, I don't know, sweetie."

"That was it, wasn't it?"

"Oh, God!"

"What is it, Oliver?"

"The pain is back."

"Oliver!"

"I'll call you," he said and gently put the phone on the hook.

Oliver invited Arf to his apartment for lunch. He wanted to report the outcome of the Brooklyn difficulty and also explain a plan he had.

"So what is it?" Arf said.

"No fucking."

"At all?"

"I've decided to cut out fucking entirely. Just take a rest and think."

"Think about what?"

"Think about what has to be thought about."

"You're going to think a lot about fucking."

"That's OK, if that's what needs thinking."

"That's what *will* need thinking. If I put you out on a desert, you'd think about water, wouldn't you? If someone turned off the air, you'd think about air."

"That's not my idea."

"What's your idea?"

"Well, I've been fucking so much I'm confused about it."

"What's to be confused? You enjoy it?"

"Most of the time."

"What do you mean, 'most of the time'?"

"Most of the time I enjoy it."

"And the rest of the time?"

"Not as much."

"So, that's like everybody."

"Then maybe everybody should take time off and think about it."

"What do you expect to learn?"

"I don't know yet."

"But you think you'll learn something?"

"Definitely."

"Are you going to play with yourself?"

"There'd be no point if I played with myself."

"So you'll go around with a hard-on. You did that when you were a kid. Did it teach you anything?"

"I'll tell you one thing: I was in love when I was a kid."

"Who with?"

"Different girls. But I was always in love."

"Was that good?"

"Yes."

"Let me ask you a question. All the girls you were in love with, would you want to be married to them today?"

"Maybe."

"Which ones?"

"It depends how they turned out."

"They turned out to be Long Island, Florida, and Brooklyn."

"Maybe that's what I want to discover."

"I just told you."

"I have to discover it for myself. Besides, you're over-simplifying everything. It's an extremely complicated subject. Every religion, for instance, teaches chastity for certain people at certain times."

"Not Jews."

"Don't they have something in the Old Testament?"

"Not that I heard of."

"You're sure?"

"If a Jew did what you're planning, he'd be considered crazy."

"But I'm not Jewish."

"That doesn't mean you're not crazy," Arf said.

The first week was encouraging. At Tuesday lunch, Oliver went with the Quiff copyboy and two editors from another of the organization's magazines to the Green Fields Pool Hall. Although he hadn't played in a month and at best his game was mediocre, Oliver had an immediate run of twenty-six balls. Through the hour and a quarter they played, he made run after run, although not one of twenty-six again. It was dreamlike. A small group of habitués gathered around the table; and once, when there was a single-bank shot, he smiled, almost imperceptibly, and took a double-bank shot that left him in a superior position. The habitués murmured, something they rarely did. Oliver's companions were so awed by the whole performance that they had missed the little smile.

Walking back to the office, the two editors and the copyboy leaned toward Oliver to hear his explanation. "All I can say is that I saw the angles. I mean, what do you do ordinarily? You *figure* the angles, but I could *see* them. It was like watching a movie. And I'll tell you something else. Each and every shot that went in I knew was going in, and every shot that didn't go in I knew was not going in. . . . Am I making it clear?" They nodded. "The whole thing was mental rather than physical. You know how, when you play chess, all you need is the idea? Well, that's all I needed, the idea."

"That's kind of profound, Mr. Bacon," the copyboy said.

When he reached his office, there was a manila house-mail envelope on Oliver's desk. Arf had sent a selection of black-and-whites from the February Whiff of Quiff shooting. Oliver had originated the theme two weeks before in a memo to Mather: "To E. M. Re Feb. Woq. Double foldout down. Front—blonde, titsy-tartsy, emerging from well-used bed; white hair of Old Year peeks from bedclothes. Reverse—same chick, now pert and douched, entering fresh empty bed, eyes inviting Reader to be New Year. O. B." These were not the Whiff shots themselves but candids that the photographer had taken as a record of the session. Among other scenes, they showed the fag prop man arranging a sheet over the model's pubic hair; the same model arching in front of the studio mirror practicing breast thrust; the same prop man in the New Year set, a grimace of urgency on his face, pointing at January's crotch and saying something. The last picture, taken apparently after the session was over, showed the model sitting on a wire-backed chair, coffee in one hand, cigarette in the other. She held half her robe away with the heel and pinky of the cigarette hand while she crossed her legs. Revealed by low-angle strobe light was her vagina, on which Arf had written in red china-marking pencil a telephone number and the words "Eat me!"

Oliver stuffed the pictures into their envelope and the envelope into the desk drawer he kept for storage, got to his feet, and went about the office looking for the watering can. He found it in the pornographic art book cabinet and watered his one plant, an old grape ivy. It soaked up the entire contents of the can. Oliver sat down again and looked over his desk for the next piece of business. Instead of attending to it, however, he took out the pictures and tried to erase Arf's writing. The photo had a mat finish, and although he could obliterate the message a red blur remained. As he worked away, the impression developed that he was wiping between the model's legs. His penis swelled to a sensitive semirigidity. Also, he had memorized the telephone number against his will. He tried to abolish it by scrambling the digits in his mind, but they returned to their places. He covered the model's genital with his hand and concentrated on her hard, bored expression; but as sometimes happened to him, he seemed to be able to see the child in the adult features.

He studied particularly the eyes and mouth and was struck by their underlying purity, a purity perverted by pain. The thought occurred to him that if he could address the girl in person and say something very, very simple, her innocence would be uncovered and renewed. But his penis began to swell further, and, after shuffling the pictures into their original order, he took them into Mather's office. Mather enjoyed all visits from his staff. No matter how busy he was, anyone could discuss anything with him. In fact, the less the topic had to do with magazine business the more pleased he was. Mather filled his head with the concerns of his colleagues; it seemed to give him a sense of union with them. Without comment Oliver handed him the pictures. Mather studied them one by one and began to smile slyly, the way people smile when being told a dirty joke. At the last picture, though, he flinched, stood up, came around his desk, pushed the photographs into Oliver's hands, and jostled him from the office, saying, "All right, all right, all right!" Oliver went back to his desk stunned. After regaining his composure he walked past Mather's office. Mather was not at his desk. With a look Oliver asked the secretary where he was. She shook her head in ignorance. Oliver went to lunch thinking that, whatever else had happened, at least the fire was out in his pants.

Thursday night, as he did occasionally, Oliver played doubles tennis on a floodlit rooftop court of a friend's apartment house. He experienced the same effect as in the pool hall. In the past his serve had always been irregular. Every now and then, for a short while and no apparent reason, a series of fine serves would burst forth, and he would deliver, say, four consecutive aces for a love game. But then, as suddenly and inexplicably, the serve would disintegrate into the usual long, short, and lob shots. He often told himself that there was a great tennis player inside struggling to get out. Thursday night it got out.

Even the sounds of his shots, hit hard in the racket's center, were impressive and satisfying. If his serves were returned, and most were not, he moved to the net as if he was not only ten feet tall but ten feet wide. After returning the opponents' serves, he rushed in with the same assurance. The other team was quickly demoralized, which only increased his feelings of mastery. It was his net game that broke their spirit completely. So keen was his judgment about where the ball would arrive that had he been playing bridge he would have been accused of cheating.

After the match, one of his opponents asked him where he had been taking lessons.

"I haven't been taking lessons."

"Come on, Ollie!"

"Yeah, Ollie," his own partner said.

"Honestly." But no one believed him.

After Monday's call from Brooklyn he had no more calls from her, Florida, or Long Island until Saturday morning, when Long Island called him at home.

"Oliver."

"Yes."

"This is Lillian."

"Lillian Bauer?"

"Yes."

"Mrs. Gus Bauer? *That* Lillian Bauer?"

"Oliver, if you want me to hang up, I will."

"Keep talking while I turn on the tape recorder."

"You're still angry with me."

"Where are you?"

"I'm home."

"I'm not angry with you. It's just that you did a stupid thing, the stupidest thing I ever heard of."

"Oh, I know, Oliver. If only I could take it back."

"You can't, sweetie."

"But it's smoothed over."

"How?"

"He confessed to something himself."

"What?"

"He also had an affair."

"See, you never know."

"And he slept with her exactly three times, too."

"Maybe he's telling you the same kind of truth you told him."

"Three times is right for him, Oliver."

"The affair lasted two years, I bet."

"A year and a half."

"And he was doing the girl a favor."

"He said that, the first time, she had just broken up with her boyfriend and needed reassurance."

"Well, all I can say, Lillian, is that things sure do work out."

". . . Oliver."

"Yes."

"I miss you terribly."

"I miss you, too, sweetie; but I'm trying to turn over a new leaf."

"What do you mean?"

"I'm practicing celibacy."

"You're *what?*"

"I've given up making love."

". . . Completely?"

"Absolutely completely."

"Did I do that to you?"

"You contributed. . . . But that's not the point. The point is I want to be alone for a while."

"Oliver, may I tell you something?"

"Sure."

"I decided to do the same thing after I told Gus."

"Have you kept it?"

Silence.

"You hopped into the sack with Gus as soon as he confessed, right?"

"Not only."

"Sweetie, I'm not your husband. You don't have to confess to me."

"I know that."

"I don't want to hear about the neighbor or the TV repairman or *anybody*."

"It doesn't concern *anybody*, it concerns . . . you."

"OK, what?"

"Yesterday, while you were at work. . . ."

"Yes?"

"I called you up."

"At the office?"

"I called you at home."

"I wasn't there."

"I know."

"So?"

"While the phone rang, I thought about you. . . ."

"Yes?"

"Oliver."

"Yes?"

"I had an orgasm."

". . . From listening to the phone?"

"A terrific orgasm. I pictured your bedroom and the bed and the sun coming in the window."

"That's fantastic."

"It was fantastic. I touched myself and I had a fantastic orgasm."

"You mean you were masturbating."

"Oh, Oliver!"

"Lillian, are you doing it now?"

"Oh, Oliver, I love you."

"Sweetie, this isn't fair. I'm trying to keep myself cool."

"All right, Oliver. All right, Oliver."

". . . Did you come?"

"Onnnh!"

"Sweetie, I have to go."

". . . All right, Oliver. I understand."

He put down the phone and walked briskly around the apartment, punching pillows, putting dirty ashtrays into the sink, opening and closing closets. When everything seemed in its place, he vacuumed the rugs; but not until he hit himself in the forehead with the bathroom door did he get rid of the picture of Long Island playing with herself by her phone.

Monday at 5:15 P.M., just as Oliver was about to leave, the receptionist called to say there was a girl to see him. "I think her name is Puerto Rico."

"Puerto Rico?"

"I think that's it. Should I get her to write it down?"

"No, send her in. What does she look like?"

"She looks a little like Joan Baez, only Puerto Rican."

"Hell, send her in!"

Oliver rose to greet the girl and motioned her to the visitor's chair. "Miss . . . ?"

"I Mees Puerto Rico. Meester Arf send me for Queef."

"I see."

"I do great things for you, Meester Arf says. I bring peectures. You like to see these? Meester Arf says I am very preetty all over."

"I'm sure you are. How does Mr. Arf know this?"

"Een my peectures. You see these?"

"Your name isn't really Puerto Rico, is it?"

"Eet ees my professional name."

"How long has it been your professional name?"

"Today Meester Arf says eet do good for me."

"How do you mean?"

"You like my name? You like to see my peectures?"

"Maybe you ought to tell me first what you want to do for the magazine."

"I like Queef. Eet ees sexy like me. You like to see my peectures? Put them in Queef? At your place? My place?"

"I tell you, Miss— What's your real name?"

"Juanita." She leaned forward and lowered her voice. "I know your trouble, Meester Bacon. I have help many man like you."

"How do you mean?"

"Meester Arf told me your trouble. I theenk I help you. You like to see my peectures. Your place? My place?"

Oliver's phone rang. It was Arf. "How do you like eet, babee?"

Oliver turned his head away, so the girl couldn't hear. "What the hell are you screwing around for?"

"I'm just trying to harden you up, baby. You're going to have a lot of temptation as time goes on, and I thought I'd harden you up a little."

"Thanks."

"And I want you always to remember what Oscar Wilde said about temptation."

"His trouble wasn't my trouble. What *is* my trouble, by the way?"

"I told her you couldn't get it up."

"You prick!"

"She says she can help you, babee."

"I'm sure she could. Has she been helping you?"

"Not yet. I might let her help me tonight if you don't want her to help you. Send her back down here if you decide no. But, baby, before you make up your mind— where is she? Is she there?"

"Not a foot away."

"Before you make up your mind, do yourself a favor and peek at the peectures. She has an absolutely perfect body. Hard little tits, hard little ass. We can't use her in the magazine—too lean—but she'd be great for action. Break your cock off."

"Arf, she's only doing this to get her picture in Quiff. You're leading the girl on."

"Oh, come on, baby! She's a pro. She's not going to be debauched by a little additional fucking."

"She'll be disappointed."

"Life is full of disappointments."

"OK, Arfie."

"So what are you going to do?"

"Don't wait around for her," Oliver said and put down the phone. He turned to the girl. "All right, miss, put your pictures away and let's go have a drink."

"Your place? My place?"

'We'll just go to a bar around the corner."

"OK, Meester Bacon."

Oliver took her to a restaurant and bar that was a favorite with magazine editors for lunch. Evenings the crowd turned to young show business types, so the girl did not look out of place. They took a booth in the rear. After ordering drinks, Oliver adopted a serious tone. "You're very nice to want to help me with my problem, Miss— What the hell is your real name, your last name?"

"Puerto Rico ees no good?"

"It's fine. It's just not your real name. I can't call you Miss Puerto Rico, as if you won a beauty contest."

"I am no good in beauty contest?"

"No, you're very pretty. It's just that. . . . I tell you what, let me call you Juanita, and you can call me Oliver. What I want to tell you is that I don't think Mr. Arf is going to use your pictures in the magazine."

"I am not preetty? You do not see my peectures."

"Boy, this is complicated, Juanita. . . .OK, do you want to hear the whole story?"

She smiled and nodded.

"A week or so ago, I decided to give up making love. Stop making love. Not forever, but for a while."

"I have done this sometime."

"Well, then you understand. And Mr. Arf sent you to tempt me. Do you understand?"

"You can make love eef you want?"

"Yes, but I've decided not to."

"Why?"

"To be alone for a while."

The girl nodded thoughtfully.

"As for Quiff, Juanita, that phone call I got when you were sitting at my desk was from Mr. Arf. He told me he wasn't going to use your pictures in the magazine. It isn't that you aren't pretty enough. He said you were very pretty. But you're too thin. For the magazine, that is. Not too thin otherwise, but too thin for the magazine. Do you understand?"

"*You* use the peectures, Meester Bacon?"

"That's not my decision, Juanita. It's Mr. Arf's decision."

"You don't see these peectures. Very sexy."

Oliver shook his head negatively. The girl made a further questioning expression, and again Oliver shook his head.

"You eat sheet."

"*What?*"

"You eat sheet," the girl said, slid from the booth and walked out of the restaurant with not even a glance back.

"What have we done about the pixshtick for Arf?" Mather asked first thing Tuesday morning.

"Were we serious about that?"

"You mean, we haven't done anything, Ollie? We

decided to move on that weeks ago. I'm a little disappointed, I don't mind telling you, and a little upset too."
There was a threatening formality in Mather's tone.

"I can whip one up in an hour, Mother."

"We can whip up an entire issue in an hour—if we're willing to sacrifice quality." Mather spoke loud, which was even more ominous. It meant he wanted the complaint on record with the rest of the staff. "I don't think we should *whip* one up at all. I'll tell you what I think we should do, I think we should *work* one up and I think we should spend more than an hour on it."

"Check!" Oliver said.

The staff was listening now. Typing had stopped; people had told phone callers that they would get back to them. Mather went on: "Oliver, this comes as a surprise to me."

"What does?"

"Simply that we make plans for a project—formalize the matter, so to speak—and then no action is taken, no action whatever. If I had known nothing would be done, I'd have given it to someone else here." Mather nodded toward two or three people at nearby desks. "Or, God knows, I'd have done it myself. Frankly, I've been waiting for your suggestions. It was only when you failed to deliver that I brought it up."

"But, Mother, I said I'd have one to you shortly."

"And I'm sure you will, Ollie. It's certainly not that you can't do it. Ollie, you're my assistant editor. If I can't rely on you, whom can I rely on?" Again he looked at other staff members.

"Honestly, Mother, I don't think it's worth all this fuss."

"All this fuss!" His voice rose again. "This magazine is my responsibility. If the issue doesn't come out, it's not you who will bear the brunt, it's I."

"Oh, for Christ's sake, when has an issue not come out?"

"The issue has always come out, Ollie; and I like to think it has because I've been in charge. And I'll tell you one more thing, Ollie. It is my function in this office to tighten the ropes when they slacken. If staff interest wanes, it's up to me to do something about it."

"My interest hasn't waned, Mother. You know that."

"Yes, I thought I did, Ollie, and I hope I was right."

The exchange would have been over, but Oliver thought for insurance he'd better launch a small counter-attack. "You know, Mother, a house shtick is going to cost a lot more than a free-lance job."

"Ollie, how can you say that?" Mather had lowered his voice almost to a whisper and stepped in between Oliver and the rest of the staff.

"We got the Caribbean treasure hunt for how much?"

"Three thousand," Mather said.

"Fifteen hundred is more like it."

"Are you sure, Ollie?"

"We can call Auditing."

"No, your memory is good enough for me, Ollie. But I don't think money itself is entirely the point."

"It always is when I want to spend it."

"The point, Ollie, is what you get for what you spend —that's the point."

"*You* said the Caribbean shtick was terrific. *I* was the one who didn't like it."

"I still maintain it was terrific and I'm confident the new one will be even better. But the point is this—something, by the way, Ollie, you would do well to keep in mind if you want to move up to more responsibility in this organization—the point is that the purchase goes beyond the material acquisition."

"I don't get you."

"I'm talking about the revivification of the staff. Suppose we do spend three or four thousand with Arf. . . ."

"*Three or four thousand!*"

"Yes, that's what I said, Ollie. Suppose we do, and by spending it we revivify the staff. The publisher would completely back me up on this."

"I still don't understand you."

"How many times have we heard Arf complain about working *in vacuo?*"

"*In vacuo!* Arf complained about working *in vacuo?*"

"Ollie, you're being picky. It's my phrase." Mather was now bending close to Oliver so that no one else could possibly overhear him. "Arf said—and I will use his words —he needs the *smell* of flesh to go on *judging* flesh."

"He probably said 'the smell of cunt.' "

"Perhaps he did. . . ."

"Mother, Arf carries a little piece of cunt around in his watch pocket to sniff when he feels faint."

"We're wandering from the point, Ollie. The point I'm trying to make is that a house shtick would be a good thing for all of us."

"All of us?"

"I expect you to come along, of course."

"Are you going?"

When anyone stood up to Mather in this fashion he softened. "Don't you think the editor needs a little revivifying too?" he said, chuckled, and put his hand on Oliver's shoulder. By conscious effort Oliver kept himself from gagging. He had an image of submitting to the nausea, turning his head, and vomiting on the hand. But Mather gave Oliver a little squeeze and returned to his office.

Oliver phoned Arf. "The old turd wants to come along on the shtick you wangled."

"That's how I wangled it, baby. I told him there'd be plenty of action. It didn't take much convincing."

"Since when does he want action?"

"I think he likes to watch it, baby."

"OK, since it's your party, do you have a shtick idea?"

"I sure do. Buzz down, and I'll spread it out for you."

As Oliver stood up, his phone rang. The receptionist told him that Miss Puerto Rico was back and this time wanted to see the editor. What should she do?

There's something for Mother to watch, Oliver thought. "Send her in and tell his secretary I suggested he see her! Just give me time to get out the back way!"

Arf's plan was to simulate the Aegean on Long Island Sound. The story line called for a yacht chartered by five young girls out for sun and rest, another yacht chartered by five young men out for sun and fun. The male boat sights the female boat and makes mating signs. The female boat flees. The male boat overtakes and attempts to board. The girls defend themselves with pillows and bathing caps. Bikini tops fall in the fray. The boarding party prevails, followed by a naked plank-walking scene. Eventually everyone settles down, more or less in pairs, to sun themselves. The few remaining tops disappear; and as soon as the sun sinks in the west, the bottoms too. "All look forward to a fulfilling evening," Arf concluded. "Where does that grab you?"

"Where does it grab Auditing?" Oliver said. "Won't there have to be a third boat to photograph from?"

"You betcha!"

"So how much will it cost?"

"Five/six."

"Mother was talking three/four."

"Mother should be glad we're letting him go. Come on over to my place tonight, and we'll work out the details."

When Oliver got back to his desk, the office was in an uproar. Mather had locked himself in his private bathroom and wouldn't tell anyone what the trouble was. The secretary turned to Oliver as second in command: "Mr. Bacon, I'm so frightened! Mr. Mather always told me to get him, *wherever he is,* if the publisher phoned. And the publisher has called twice. The second time he sounded peeved. He said, 'If Mather's there, tell him this is urgent! If he's not at his post, admit it!' "

"What did you say?"

"To Mr. Mather?"

"The publisher."

"I told him Mr. Mather was at his post in the bathroom and was indisposed."

"Did you tell Mother the publisher called?"

"Only the first time. It was terrible. He moaned."

"He moaned?"

"He moaned. I pleaded with him to let me call Medical, but he said it would cost me my job if I did. Oh, Mr. Bacon, I don't know what to do."

"I'll take care of it," Oliver said. "Get everyone out of there!"

The secretary cleared Mather's office. Oliver went in and closed the door. Standing near the bathroom, he said in a low voice, "Mother!"

Silence.

"Mother, this is Oliver. What's up?"

"Nothing."

"The publisher wants to talk to you."

"Where is he? Is he here?"

"No, he phoned."

"O–o–o–o!"

"What's the matter with you?"

"Find out what he wants!"

"What'll I say about you?"

"Better not. I'll call him when I get out."

"Let me get Medical."

"No Medical!"

"What's the matter with you?"

"Take over the ship! Till I get back on deck, take over the ship!"

"Don't you want me to stay here in case you get worse? Why can't you tell me what's the matter?"

"The ship, the ship! Take over the ship! That's an order."

As Oliver closed the door to Mather's office, he thought with a little thrill of pleasure how like pulling a sheet over a dead man's face it was. He reassured the staff to the extent that they were concerned—there was more curiosity than concern—and took up the magazine's business. There were no more calls from the publisher. At one o'clock, when the staff left for lunch, Oliver knocked on Mather's door.

Mather was sitting at his desk, white and worried.

"You OK, Mother?"

"Yes, I am. I've left word with the publisher's secretary to call me as soon as he returns. You can go to lunch now, and leave the door open!"

That evening at Arf's, Oliver narrated the story.

"And you have no idea what was wrong?"

"None."

"Get on the extension!" Arf said, pointing to the phone in the hall. "I'll call from the bedroom." They could see one another through the bedroom doorway.

"Mother, baby, how are you?"

"Who's this?"

"It's Arfie, baby. How's the old Mother? Heard you had a little thing in there today."

"Where did you hear that?"

"All around the shop, baby."

"From whom?"

"Everybody."

"Who is everybody?"

Oliver, pointing to himself, shook his head. Arf held up his hand in reassurance.

"Everyone was talking about it, Mother. Anyway, how the hell are you?"

"I'm quite well, Arf. But I'd like to know just who was talking and precisely what was said."

"Well, let's see. I got most of it from Lou Prepobotzo. You know Lou?"

"No. What department is he in?"

Oliver mouthed the question "Who?" and Arf shrugged his shoulders.

"Old Lou Prepobotzo, in Promotion."

"I don't know him. What did he say?"

"He said you were holed up in your can half the day. Everybody banging on the door. You moaning inside like crazy. You wouldn't let anyone get Medical. It sounded like a circus."

"It was no circus, Arf; and that report is wildly exaggerated. I was away from my desk for one hour, no more."

"Jesus, I'm glad to hear that, Mother. I thought it was your *Herz.*"

"My *what?*"

"Your heart, baby."

"Heart! I don't have heart trouble."

"Well, you're what, Mother? Fifty? No one could figure out why you wouldn't talk about it."

"How do you know I didn't talk about it?"

"I heard."

"Ollie told you."

"Lou Prepobotzo told me."

"Who told him?"

"Was it your stomach, Mother?"

"It was not. . . . Well, in a sense, it was. A little stomach upset, of a sort."

"That's good news, Mother. I mean, not the heart. So you have stomach trouble."

"I don't have stomach *trouble,* Arf. I'm in excellent health. What happened to me yesterday was an illusion."

"A stomach illusion?"

"It was the work of the imagination."

"For Christ's sake! Imagine that!"

"It's an old story, really. It passed before and it will pass again."

"An old story! For Christ's sake!"

"That sounds worse than it is, Arf. Actually it amounts to nothing. It's just damned discomforting."

"Discomforting. Tsk!"

"It's so minor, it hardly warrants discussion."

Arf remained silent and to Oliver held up his left thumb and index finger in a circle.

"I'll tell you exactly what it amounts to, Arf. It's a feeling. . . ."

"Yes."

"A feeling . . . that I'm about to soil myself."

"Very common," Arf said.

"I don't know how common it is, but it's certainly unpleasant."

"When you say soil yourself, do you mean number-two-wise?"

"Of course. Otherwise I'd have said wet myself."

"Of course. But you said it was an old story. It happened before?"

"Many times. And it has always passed."

"Like many times when, Mother?"

"It happened today and yesterday. But the last time before that was eleven years ago, on a Fifth Avenue bus. I rushed off, into the Hotel Pierre. I couldn't find a bathroom for the life of me. I never thought I'd make it."

"But you did."

"Oh, yes. I always make it. In fact, when I get there, the feeling disappears. It's when I start to go out that the feeling comes back."

"That sounds shitty, Mother. Is that what happened today? And you say yesterday?"

"Yes. It was terribly disturbing. The publisher called."

"Twice."

"*Twice?*"

"That's what Prepobotzo said."

"O–o–o–o! He never called back. Do you think I should phone him at home?"

"Mother, relax! Tomorrow is another day."

"Yes, yes, it is. It certainly is."

They were both silent for a few seconds, then Mather said, "Arf, I hope you will keep this to yourself."

"Mother! Of course! Mother, let me ask you something. What brings the feeling on?"

"That's it, Arf. I have no idea."

"And when does it finally go?"

"When it's justified."

"How do you mean?"

"Well, when the feeling is justified, I . . . act upon it; and that in turn purges the feeling. It has its own logic, you see."

"You mean you crap and then you don't feel like crapping anymore."

"Exactly."

"Nature is very peculiar, isn't it?"

"Yes, it is, Arf, and sometimes very disagreeable too."

Again they were silent. Then Mather said, "Arf, this whole subject brings up another matter that's been on my mind."

"Shoot!"

"Have you—and be frank!—noticed anything about Ollie lately?"

"Jesus, it's funny you should mention that. I certainly have. Tell me what you're thinking about!"

"Well, you know how close I've been to Ollie."

"I certainly do, Mother."

"Almost like a father."

"Exactly like a father."

"Well, I'm worried about him."

"Two minds with but a single thought, Mother. That's all I can say, because I've been worried too, worried as hell."

"So you've noticed it."

"I have. Tell me what *you* noticed!"

"Yesterday he did the strangest thing."

"Yes."

"He brought in some black-and-whites of the Whiff session."

"Yes."

"On one of them, in red pencil, he drew. . . ."

"Yes."

"He drew blood."

"He drew *blood,* Mother?"

"*Menstrual* blood."

"Oliver did *that?*"

"Yes. I think the boy is in trouble."

"I'll say! Did he tell you why he did it?"

"Nothing. No explanation. He just handed me the pictures."

"Tsk, tsk! That's bad trouble."

"And today."

"Yes."

"Today he sent a whore in to see me, a common little Spanish whore."

"Why did he do that, Mother?"

"This will sound strange, Arf."

"Go ahead!"

"I believe he did it to upset me."

"That doesn't surprise me."

"It *is* like him, isn't it, Arf?"

"I can only say this because I'm very close to Ollie too, almost like a big brother; but, yes, it does sound like him. Let me ask you something, Mother, because I feel I know Ollie, and he's a very ambitious boy. . . . Do you think he's after your . . . job?"

"I'd hate to think that, Arf; but there's something going on there. You know what he did about the pixshtick after we agreed that you should do one?"

"What did he do, Mother?"

"Nothing. Absolutely nothing. He was going to let it die. I'd call that jealousy, wouldn't you?"

"I'm afraid I would call it jealousy. Which makes me very sad, and a little angry. That was a lousy thing to do, *lousy*."

"It was *destructive*," Mather said.

Again they were silent. Then Arf said, "I hate to say this, Mother. . . ."

"Go ahead, Arf, speak your mind!"

"I think the time has come . . . to cut Ollie Bacon down to size."

"Exactly!" Mother said.

Again silence. Then Mather said, "I think we should both think about this, Arf."

"I'm going to think about it very hard, Mother."

"Arf."

"Yes, Mother."

"I want to thank you for . . . your interest in me and my little upset."

"Just ordinary human concern for a friend and colleague."

"And, Arf. . . ."

"Yes."

"I think our little talk has done me good."

"Kind of a catharsis?"

"Exactly! . . . Good night, Arf!"

"Good night, Mother!"

Arf hung up first, then Oliver. They sat at opposite ends of the apartment looking at one another like two teammates after the game. "Drinks first!" Arf said and went to the kitchen. Oliver settled down in the living room. They sipped their drinks for a few minutes before talking, then discussed the reason for Mather's hostility to Oliver, deciding it was due to complicated and as yet undefinable causes. They discussed Oliver's hostility to Mather and decided it was justified because he was "a shit." Apparently sight of the Whiff picture had also sent Mather to the bathroom the day before, and they decided his symptoms were due to "sexual anxiety." The only strategy they evolved was "to get the old turd laid" on the pixshtick. Otherwise Arf would stay in touch with Mather and keep Oliver up on his plans. "And you better be nice to me, baby," Arf added. Oliver left for home at five thirty in the morning.

The shtick was scheduled for fifteen people and budgeted at between four and five thousand dollars.

An Old-Fashioned Darling

There were to be five female and four male models, whose services Arf was to get for a hundred and fifty dollars a model. He pointed out to the agency that Quiff had been very good to them in the past and also that everyone would be accorded "the best of accommodations available." The Quiff copyboy agreed to act as a male model "in exchange," as Arf put it, "for the ride." The photographer, a wet-lipped young Englishman named Derek, accompanied by his assistant, a wide-eyed girl named Yoyo, would ordinarily have gotten fifteen hundred dollars for a weekend traveling job; but Arf, hinting at more lucrative work in the future, got him down to a thousand. At four hundred dollars Arf engaged eight units in the Hampton Plaza Motel for Friday and Saturday nights, breakfasts included. Friday and Saturday supper and a late lunch Sunday were arranged at Chez Mario for five dollars per meal per person, one drink included. Box lunches for the actual shoot Chez Mario would also provide for two fifty apiece. Three rented station wagons were expected to come to two hundred and fifty dollars, and a hundred was put aside for "miscellaneous booze."

Arf had most of his difficulty with the boats. Two of them had to look as if they slept five in luxury, and the third had to be fast and maneuverable enough to get the photographer to good vantage points for the engagement, flight, and boarding. Arf's first inquiry, to the Yachting Club of America, brought an estimate of seven thousand dollars for vessels and crews. "I'm not shooting the Spanish Armada, baby. I just want a few Kodachromes with no pubic hair showing." Finally through a chain of acquaintances he was put in touch with the manager of a marina near Sag Harbor, who seemed to understand what was needed and promised to deliver it for fourteen hundred dollars. Thursday Arf took a helicopter out to look at the boats. "What if it rains Saturday?" the marina man said.

"We'll shoot Sunday."

"What if it rains Sunday?"

"We'll shoot ourselves, OK?"

"OK with me," the man said.

Friday afternoon, when the party drove out, the forecast was excellent. It looked as if there would be typical September weather—warm sun, cool shade, west winds, blue skies. On arrival at the Hampton Plaza, Arf told the group to distribute themselves in pairs of their own choosing among six of the eight apartments. He and Oliver would take one, and Mr. Mather would have one to himself. ("We'll keep him unattached until we find the right attachment," Arf had said to Oliver.) At seven o'clock the group walked a quarter of a mile to Chez Mario, where they were almost the only guests and were served chicken cacciatore. After dinner, everyone went his own way—there was a nearby movie and a roadside tavern called the Sandbar. Arf, Oliver, and Mather returned to Arf and Oliver's room. Arf immediately opened a bottle of scotch, and Oliver got a bag of ice from a machine next to the motel office. Oliver settled down against the headboard of one bed, Mather against the headboard of the other, and Arf sat in a stuffed chair with a sketch pad on his knees.

"Shouldn't the photographer be here?" Oliver said.

"That creepy girl assistant would come along," Arf said.

"What's the matter with her?"

"She's creepy."

"I think she's kind of cute."

"You do? I asked her," Arf said, "what her name stood for, and she said it stood for the toy."

"The toy?"

"Her father was yo-yo champ of Ohio and he named her for the toy."

"I still think she's cute."

"Baby, you're hitting that phase where everything is cute. I saw you eyeing one of the male models at dinner."

"What phase is Ollie hitting?" Mather said.

Oliver frowned at Arf and gave a quick shake of his head, which Mather noticed. "No, Ollie, I'd like to know what Arf meant by that."

"Oliver here has given up fucking," Arf said.

"I'd like to hear about that," Mather said, sitting upright. "Would you like to talk about it, Ollie?"

"Not particularly."

"I don't mean to pry, Ollie, but that *is* an extraordinary thing for a young man to do."

Oliver said nothing. Arf smiled.

"Celibacy has a long and honored tradition," Mather said.

"That's what he told me himself when he announced the plan," Arf said.

"How long has this been going on, Ollie?"

Arf answered for him. "Two weeks."

"You've just begun. I take it you had a rather active sex life before. Have you noticed any changes during the two weeks?"

"No."

"No heightening of the muscle tone?" Arf said, "no increase in perceptive powers? Didn't you tell me your tennis game improved?"

"You must be experiencing a sense of privation," Mather said.

"Some."

"He has trouble pissing through his perpetual hard-on," Arf said.

"What interests me most, Ollie," Mather went on, "is the reason. Why did you make such a resolve? You're not religious, are you?"

"No"

"Is it then simply a task you've set yourself, like climbing a mountain?"

"Somewhat."

"If I may ask, how long do you plan to continue?"

"I have no plans, Mother."

"You want to see what will happen?"

"Yes."

"It's sort of a personal experiment."

"Yes, personal."

"Well, frankly, Oliver, I find it fascinating, and I also think it helps explain something about you lately."

"Like what?" Oliver said, sitting upright himself.

"Ah-ha-*ha!*" Mather said. "I have eyes."

"Oh, for Christ's sake!"

"I have, Ollie. But just let's leave it at that," Mother said and reached over to tap Oliver on the knee.

As Arf and Oliver went on discussing the project, Mather had less and less to say and after a while seemed hardly to listen, although he smiled and nodded occasionally. He was regularly helping himself to the scotch, so that before the evening was over Arf had to open a second bottle. Arf made cartoons of the photographs he expected to get. "And if it takes another turn, let it." Oliver asked again whether the photographer Derek shouldn't be present, at least listening to them talk. "No, no, no!" Arf said. "I want spontaneity, vitality, verve. Anyway, if we get him here he'll want to run the whole show."

At eleven thirty the phone rang. Oliver answered it. "Arf, female."

"Hi. . . . Oh, hi. . . . Yes. . . . Not yet. . . . Un-huh. . . . Yep. . . . Well. . . . Yep. . . . Right. . . . Yeah, sure. . . . Right. . . . Call you in a minute." He hung up and went over to Mather, who was flat on his back now, head to one side, saliva trickling from the corner of his mouth. Arf shook one leg. No response. "You know who that was?"

"Who?"

"Lois."

"Who's Lois?"

"The model. The little brunette with the **big tits**. We have an arrangement for tonight."

"Yeah?"

"But she has a roommate."

"Are you going to screw the roommate too?"

"Lois doesn't go for that. Anyway, Lois—that's my pussycat—claims that Beryl—that's your pussycat. . . ."

"*My* pussycat!"

"Now listen to the whole thing, will you?"

"The answer is no."

"Listen, will you? Beryl noticed you and digs you."

"When did she notice me?"

"When we were loading up in the city and at dinner tonight."

"And she digs me."

"That's what she told Lois. She was on my left, the little blonde with the big tits. Do you know which one I mean?"

"It makes no difference. If you want to go over there, go; but I don't want her here."

"Nothing so crude as that. I thought the four of us would get together for a few drinks and see how everybody likes everybody."

"No sale."

"You won't even look?"

"No."

"Even if it means fucking it up for me?"

"Love will find a way."

"Look, Ollie, I think your little experiment is great. Clears the complexion and everything. But why don't you begin again on Monday?"

"Because I don't want to begin again on Monday. If I begin again on Monday, there'd be no reason why I couldn't turn it off every Friday and begin again every Monday. Anyway, I thought you wanted to get *him* laid. Why don't you put the girl on *him?*"

"Ollie, this is not a whore. Beryl is not a whore. She's got to meet the guy and like him."

"Well, bring her over and let her have a look. I'll wipe the spit off the bedspread. And I'll tell you something else, I did not appreciate you talking about my personal business to him."

"But, baby, he likes you again. He thinks you're *fascinating.*"

"I *still* didn't appreciate it."

"Ah, baby, I'm sorry. I didn't mean to embarrass you. If that's what's bothering you, baby, don't let it! I mean, what do you care what a creep like that thinks, as long as he doesn't make bad noises your way?"

"It's just my business, and I don't want him knowing it."

"You're right, you're right. It was stupid, and I apologize."

"OK, let's forget it."

"So how about it?"

"The roommate?"

"Yeah, I have to call and tell her."

"Tell her no."

"You realize you're insulting the girl."

"I apologize."

"Boy, you really are something."

"That's right."

"You saw how interested Mother was in your experiment, didn't you?"

"So?"

"Baby, you two are kin spirits. How much difference is there between someone who doesn't want to do it and someone who can't?"

"Quite a lot, I'd say."

"In one case the no comes from the conscious, in the other it comes from the unconscious. Outside, it looks the same. And the reason you didn't want me to talk about it in front of Mother is that you got a look at how creepy you're being."

"You done?"

"Have you considered that maybe the reason you're giving it up is that it's about to give you up?"

"Not until now."

"Well, why don't you consider it?"

"OK, I've considered it. I'd like to go to bed."

"You know, Ollie, sometimes you can be a little shit."

"I know. So let's start moving him out of here before I take a poke at you."

"Wait! Leave him here! Beryl can spend the night in *his* room. You can't object to *that*."

"I can, but OK."

"Great! In the morning we'll tell him we couldn't budge him."

"He'll probably start puking in the middle of the night."

"A small sacrifice for an old buddy. OK, let me call Lois. . . . Lois hon, Oliver is not feeling well. He's just not up to it. Stomach, headache, feels lousy. . . . To make matters worse, Mr. Mather has passed out here. . . . Scotch. Now the plan—get this!—is for Mather to stay here with Ollie, and Beryl can go to Mather's room. . . . She'll have the whole place to herself, the boss' own room. . . . Right. . . . OK, ask her!" Arf waited, tapping his stockinged foot on the linoleum. "Yes, hon. . . . Yes. . . . Afraid? Of what? The place is full of people. . . . Yes. . . . I believe that." Arf covered the mouthpiece and told Oliver that Beryl never slept alone. "Yes. . . . Well, look, baby, she can stay with us. . . . We'll wait till she's asleep. . . . What do you mean? I had no such idea. Do you think I'm some kind of pervert or something?" Arf made a face of mock innocence for Oliver. "I'm doing my best, Lois. It's you that's standing in the way of progress. . . . Yes. . . . Yes. . . . OK, I'll ask him." Arf covered the mouthpiece. "Lois wants to know if Beryl can stay here with you as a friend."

"No."

"He said he's afraid Beryl will catch what he's got." Arf covered the mouthpiece. "God forbid!" he said and uncovered it. "Look, Lois, ask Beryl if she'll stay with Mather. . . . I know. . . . I know he's unappealing. But he's out like a light. Also, between you and me, I don't think he could make it sober. . . . Wait! Don't ask her, tell her! Tell her it's the only solution! Otherwise we'll ship her back to the city tomorrow and shoot the story without her. Go ahead, tell her!"

"You're a very romantic fella, Arf."

"In a world of creeps, baby, this is what you've got to

do. The whole thing could have been beautiful. But you want to be alone, Beryl doesn't want to be alone, Lois wants to be alone with me." Arf directed his attention to the phone. "Yeah. . . . OK, it's settled. Now wait a minute, and I'll tell you which room she should go to. We don't want old Beryl busting in on old sick Oliver." He covered the phone. "Do you want to move to Mother's room, or do we move him?"

"Move him."

"Lois, tell Beryl to go to room two in ten minutes! Mr. Mather will be tucked away safe and sound. She'll have nothing to worry about either from Mather or the boogey man. . . .OK. Now I'll come over to your place as soon as I hear her going into Mather's. . . . Where is it? Right next door. . . . No, I'm not interested in Beryl. . . . I won't even see her. . . . I have absolutely no interest in her. . . . What more can I tell you? . . . OK. . . . OK. . . . Yes, me too. . . . Mmm!" He blew a kiss into the phone and hung up. "Sometimes I wonder if it's worth it. If I were a little older I might give your experiment a try."

Oliver looked at him to see if he was serious. "I'm not proselytizing, Arf, but some strange things have been happening to me." As they lifted Mather to his feet, Oliver explained how his pool game had improved too. "Also, I can think better."

"How?"

"I can see things more clearly. I can see things as they really are. Turn him around! Drag him backwards so his knees don't buckle!"

"I don't understand—see things more clearly?"

"I'll hold him, you open the door! Like your little rendezvous tonight. Ordinarily I would have said OK; and maybe it would have been OK, or great, or sort of great. But then tomorrow comes, and what do I see? Petulance. That petulant look, that I've-been-fucked-again-and-you-did-it look. Or that other I-think-I'm-going-to-love-you-more-than-I've-loved-anybody look. What do you do with that look?"

They were in front of the door to Mather's room. "You hold him this time! And I'm not even talking about knocking the girl up, or anything dramatic like that. I'm talking about the little, draggy, everyday things. It's locked. Christ. Is the key in his pocket? Hold him! Or getting crabs. I'm talking about all the bullshit, listening to all the bullshit. Here it is! Jesus, he's slobbered all over himself. As things stand I'll go to sleep in a few minutes. I'll wake up tomorrow without a worry in the world. I'll go for a boat ride. I'll do my job. I'll get sunburned. We'll drive back Sunday. I have three Brahms records at home I want to hear. What's the matter with that?"

They laid Mather diagonally across one of the twin beds. "Lift him up a little, while I get the blanket out!" Arf said. "The trouble with you is you take fucking too seriously. You ought to look at it like eating. You need it, you enjoy it, you don't worry about it. Those girls you were fucking—at least the two married ones—they weren't making any demands on you. They just liked to screw. You had a good thing going. What you're doing now is putting yourself in an impossible position. Would you give up eating because you didn't like some of the waiters and grocery clerks?"

"I can't explain it, Arf. I haven't even thought it out completely. It just feels like the thing to do at this time."

"How do you get to sleep at night? Doesn't the old whacker stand up and ask what's happening?"

"That's the funny thing. When I was screwing around, in between the action I'd be all set for more action."

"Fucking leads to fucking."

"And no fucking leads to no fucking."

"Is that good?"

"It's . . . toning."

"Does it tone your head?"

"It *clears* my head, Arf. Arf, I want to be able to *see* people. I want to be able to *love* people."

"You sound like you want to be God, for Christ's sake."

"Look, Brooklyn was a pain in the ass. She shouldn't have been. That was my fault. She was just a girl trying to make out in life. I mean, presumably she even loved me. But I was fucking her—in the bad way as well as the good way. I should have *loved* her. I was making the *motions* of love and the *sounds* of love, but she was just a pain in the ass. . . ."

There was a knock at the door.

"Oh, Jesus, she's here," Oliver said. "Is there another way out?"

"Take it easy!" Arf said and with exaggerated calm walked to the door and opened it.

"Come in, honey! We were just putting Mr. Mather

to bed. It'll be about five more minutes. Come in and meet Oliver! Oliver, this is Beryl."

She nodded to Oliver. "I'd rather come back, Mr. Arf."

"OK, honey." Arf closed the door. "Baby, you're missing something. Those titties look like kingsize marshmallows. And did you see that round little ass? Lois said she's a dancer. Tear your cock off. Are you sure you don't want to change your mind? I could call Lois and tell her you're feeling better. Beryl would be complimented. She'd think you took a look and changed your mind."

"You weren't listening to me at all, Arf."

"I was listening."

They stripped Mather to his underwear and socks and covered him with sheet and blanket. Arf carefully put away his clothes and shoes, folded the bedspread, and generally tidied up. Finally he turned out all the lights but one lamp, the farthest illumination from Mather's bed. They left the door slightly ajar and went to their own room.

As Oliver got ready for bed, Arf stood by the window listening for Beryl. By the time she came, Oliver was in bed.

"OK, baby, everything's squared away."

Oliver from his bed could hear the muffled sounds of Beryl in the next room.

"In case you get a yen during the night, I'll leave you this," Arf said and dangled a motel key.

"What's that?"

"The key to Mother's room."

"Take it with you!"

"I'm leaving it right here, baby." Arf let the key fall noisily onto the glass bureau top and hurried from the room. Oliver jumped out of bed, snatched the key, and ran to the door. Arf was ten feet away. Oliver threw the key after him, went back into the room, and closed the door. As he was getting into bed, Arf appeared at the window and in a loud whisper said through the screen, "It's right outside your door, baby."

Oliver left the night light on and decided to attend consciously to a resolution, or at least a definition, of the possible problems before they arose. How difficult was it going to be to get to sleep? Had he drunk enough to put him out? Sounds from the other room had stopped— she probably had her shoes off—but if they started again would it be possible to change them imaginatively into, say, sounds from a television set? Would it be better to leave the light on or turn it off? Before he answered any of these questions, however, he fell asleep.

Some time later he was half awakened by what seemed to be air-raid sirens. There were added sounds—thumpings and possibly voices in distress. The Russians were attacking America! In a sudden revelation he understood that the apparent disagreements between the Russians and the Chinese had been faked to lull the West into a false sense of security. At this end of Long Island there were no underground hiding places to speak of—ten-foot cellars, but what good were they? Perhaps it was best to stay where he was. How ironic if he was the only one to survive because he had stayed in bed! On account of a geographic quirk, the shock waves and fire storms would pass around his bed. As he tried to come fully awake he recalled figures he had read about the radius of nuclear bomb destruction. A hundred miles? If it was less and all New York bombs were dead on target, he might get through. There wasn't much chance of them all being direct hits, though. Suppose one landed in the water. Would there be a tidal wave? Should he try to get inland? How wide was the island here? Fifteen miles? He should then go seven and a half miles in. Once there, should he take to a hill and chance the blast? Or stick to the lowland and chance the water? The sirens stopped. Maybe it was all a bad dream.

"Mr. Bacon, Mr. Bacon!"

Oh, God! Long Island! Gus had thrown her out after all. She must have found out where he was through an emergency call to Quiff. And now, catastrophe following catastrophe, just as she arrives at the Hampton Plaza Motel, the Russians attack. Well, at least he won't die alone. He'll die in her arms, perhaps while making love —to the most beautiful woman he has ever seen. He will hold off the orgasm until the explosion. Flash will precede impact. He will release himself into her as the blow strikes. He struggled to loose himself from the bedclothes. He must be quick. She mustn't despair of finding him and leave. As he hurried to the door, his heart pounding from the multiple excitements, he realized that Long Island would hardly have called him Mr. Bacon. He opened the door.

"May I come in?" It was Beryl. She stood wrapped in a

blanket, looking like a child. She must have been wearing high heels before. But Quiff models are always short. Tits and stuff look bigger.

"Jesus, calm in!"

"I know you'd rather be alone, Mr. Bacon, but I can't stay in that room another minute."

"You don't have to expleen."

She remained outside. "I want you to know why I'm here. I don't want any misunderstandings."

"OK, explain inseed!"

Beryl tightened the bedclothes and stepped in with dignity.

"How about a drink?"

She paused. Apparently she wanted one but didn't want to accept it.

"I'll get you a drink. I just woke up from a neatmire. The air was full of sirens."

"That was Mr. Mather moaning."

"What happened? Sit down!"

She sat in the stuffed chair. "I'm a complete wreck. I haven't been to sleep all night."

"What time is it?"

"After four."

"Jesus!"

"Right from the start he made gurgling noises. I thought he was dying. I kept getting up to see. Then he began turning and tossing—and grunting. Grunting things like 'boo' and 'anh-anh.' Then he woke up. I was facing the other way, so I couldn't actually see him. But

I could feel him standing over me. I didn't move. I made out I was asleep. I was terribly frightened."

"I'll bet you were," Oliver said and handed her a drink.

"He stood there forever. I could hear him breathing. It got louder and louder, and quicker and quicker. I didn't know what he was going to do."

"Actually you were probably pretty safe."

"You think so? That man could be a *maniac*."

"You're right, you're right."

"Well, suddenly he rushed into the bathroom. Then the moaning started. I asked him if I could help or get a doctor. But that only made it worse. Finally it stopped. He could be lying dead on the floor in there."

"Don't worry! He's not. Anyway, you poor kid!" Oliver poured more scotch into her glass to replace the little she had drunk. She was about to sip it but started to cry. This made her look to Oliver even more like a child, except for the swell of her breasts under the blanket she held. The weeping grew deeper. Oliver's body yearned to comfort her in some way. Crouch down in front of her and take her shoulders in his hands. Sit on the arm of her chair and put one hand on her cheek. Kneel and press her face against his. Lift her to her feet and take her into his arms. Pick her up like a baby and rock her to and fro.

Instead he rose briskly from the bed, on which he had been sitting, pulled the spread from the other bed with a flourish, turned back the sheet and blanket, plumped the pillow, and said, "Beryl, you need sleep. Just get in here and forget about everything! Tomorrow is another day." He plumped the pillow again; and Beryl stood up, leaving her blanket in the stuffed chair. She came to the bed like an obedient child. She wore two-piece white silk pajamas, under which her breasts were extraordinarily prominent. In her distress she seemed unconscious of her figure, and Oliver was suffused with tenderness for her. It felt like one of the fullest emotions he had ever experienced. He *loved* this little girl. He almost lost his breath. They both got into their beds simultaneously. Oliver switched off the light on the night table between them. Beryl's weeping turned to an occasional sob, and then one final sigh. Oliver was sure she had fallen asleep.

He turned on his side away from her. Soon, however, he envisioned his body and hers in perfect symmetry, back to back, knees pulled up, arms folded on chests. Although there were perhaps five feet between them, he seemed to feel the heat from her body on the back of his body. It increased. He turned to his other side, but immediately became aware of how they fit—if, in fact, she was on her side facing away from him. He tried lying on his back; but now he had an erection; and, unless he kept his knees up, it poked into the bedclothes. "Oh, God! Oh, God!" he began saying to himself. Finally it seemed to him that he had no alternative left. He lifted back his covers. As he rose from the bed, his penis came through the pajama fly. It led him like a taut leash. Gently he lifted the near side of Beryl's covers. She lay on her side away from him, just as he had imagined, knees up and arms folded on her chest. The faint light through the window made her seem violet. He thought that the instant he touched her body he would come. Would she then be aroused and he satisfied? Oh, no! he said to himself. He had ten, fifty, a hundred erections left in him. They would arrive one after the other, enough to make love to Beryl, Lois, everyone. "Everyone!" he inadvertently said aloud and lifted one leg onto her bed. Immediately Beryl awoke and scrambled away to the far side, taking the bedclothes with her. "Oh, God! Oh, God!" he thought she said. She stumbled to the door, fumbled with the lock, opened it, and ran out. His erection not only disappeared, the cool night air soon diminished his penis to less than its normal size. He poured himself a drink and sat on the edge of his bed to think.

After a time, Oliver heard scratching sounds at the window. Because of weariness, drink, and poor light, he wasn't sure what he saw. A beast seemed to be peering in. Curiosity had made it turn its head sideways; its immense mouth was vertical. Was it an unknown or rare species, something that had crawled out of the sea? It moved back and forth against the screen. Was it panting, purring? Was it a pig? If it was a wild pig, it would be dangerous. Was the screen strong enough to keep it out? Should he lock himself in the bathroom, cry for help, try to frighten it away? In panic he ran to the window and threw the contents of his drink at it. The ice cubes fell back from the screen to the floor, but the liquid passed through. Instantly Mather, naked, stood up straight, took a desperate look back, and disappeared into his room. He had apparently been rubbing his ass against the screen. Oliver couldn't have been mistaken: he heard Mather's door open and close and footfalls inside Mather's room. Oliver slammed the window shut, dropped the blind, and locked the door. He poured another drink and went into the bathroom to see what he looked like. He looked white and shocked, and his face seemed to change—grow vague and sharp and vague again. After a while he went back to bed, watched the light of dawn through the slits of the blind, and fell asleep.

"I knew you'd turn rapist," Arf said, standing over Oliver's bed.

Oliver opened his eyes. "How did you get in?"

"It's time to get up, baby."

"How did you get in?"

"With a key. This is my room. Am I a disappointment? Did you expect her to come back?"

"Who?"

"Beryl."

"Did she go to your room?"

"She sure did."

"What did she say?"

"She didn't say anything. She was hysterical."

"She didn't say anything?"

"Later she did. Later she told us the whole thing."

"Like what?"

"You tried to climb in on top of her."

"I tried to climb in *beside* her."

"That's different?"

"Yes."

"Anyway, congratulations!"

"On what?"

"On trying."

"Nothing happened."

"At least you tried, baby. You could have had it if you played it any other way."

"I know that."

"And I'll tell you something else."

"What?"

"You missed something great."

"What do you mean?"

"Very great."

"What are you talking about?"

"Beryl, baby."

Oliver stood up and hit the heel of his right hand against Arf's left shoulder. It was a solid blow, and as Arf stepped back with its impact, Oliver felt that it had been exactly balanced between play and anger. He followed with another blow to Arf's other shoulder, then a third and fourth, alternating shoulders. Arf said, "Come on! Come on!" the blows knocking emphasis into the words. With each blow Arf almost lost his balance but not quite, and in this way Oliver moved him to the doorway, there turned him around by the arms, and, fingertips to the middle of his back, pushed him outside.

The encounter not only brought Oliver wide awake, it consoled him for the night's discomfort. As he shaved, the sunlight falling on the figured, translucent paper pasted to the window made the bathroom glow. Light shone upward from the pink tile floors and white enamel sink to illuminate his features from below. As he stripped away the lather with his razor he was surprised and pleased that the night had left no marks. His face seemed fresh. As far as he could remember he had never used the word beautiful about himself; but now his green eyes, lit, it seemed, from inside, were actually beautiful. Suddenly the window paper turned gray. He waited for the cloud to pass, but it didn't. He switched on the bathroom light. Nothing but cold water came from the shower.

Breakfast consisted of grapefruit juice, sugared doughnuts, and the makings of instant coffee, laid out along a cardboard table in the motel office on a serve-yourself basis with paper plates and plastic cups and spoons. The table was messy with spilled sugar and liquids and with crumbs. Except for Oliver, the office was empty. The others stood in the motel yard around the station wagons. Oliver, sipping coffee, watched through the picture window. Arf was talking; and beside him, adding the authority of his presence, stood Mather, one hand holding the other in front of his fly. He was dressed in brown slacks and a brown, short-sleeved shirt; a new yachting cap sat on his head, emphasizing its enormous size and the thickness of the neck. In sports clothes Mather's body looked spindly and freakish. There was a faint bulge in the seat of the brown slacks.

The sky was now widely overcast. The flat light brought out a lumpiness in Beryl's face Oliver had not noticed the night before; and her figure, in slacks and tie-front blouse, seemed exaggerated beyond voluptuousness. Derek, the photographer, shifted from foot to foot, glanced up at the sky, down at his watch, down at the ground, around at the motel structures, peered in at Oliver, examined his cameras, pulled his nose, adjusted his belt. His assistant, Yoyo, stood by impassively. Lois affected a professionally serious stance, nodding occasionally at what Arf was saying. Oliver pushed the office door open to hear.

". . . spontaneity, boys and girls. Derek here says he can compensate somewhat for the lack of sunlight; but no lens trickery, let me repeat, no lens trickery can compensate for lack of spontaneity. No filmic sleight-of-hand can make up for bad acting. And that's what we'll all be doing out there today—acting. Boys and girls, we've moved this show onto location because we want to push the pixshtick to unparalleled heights. And to do this I need actors on those yachts today. . . . All right, let's go over one or two points again. The ladies will cast off first, the gents fifty yards behind. We need, Derek, pictures of both boats with wakes. But in the close-ups the boats will be at rest. You must, I repeat, must give the impression of movement. With your faces, with your bodies. There'll be a breeze, maybe a wind. Ladies, let your hair all hang out! Look dreamily over the side, dreamily at the horizon! Shade your eyes from the sun, whether there is a sun or not! Now it might get very chilly out there, but you must appear warm, you must look like you're being caressed, I repeat, caressed by the Greek sunshine. Think of Jackie and Ari, girls! Smiling, dreamy, contented. Not a care in the world. Where are you bound for? Anywhere, everywhere. It doesn't matter, this is the vacation of a lifetime. Now, the boys will also be shot in this, let's call it flaccid, state. Ah, but suddenly they spot the prize. Ship ahoy! Ship to the starboard! Talk! Gesture! Point! Move to the front of the boat! Scramble! Laugh! Anticipate!" Arf broke off and directed his attention outside the group. "Let's shake it, Warren, let's move that cute little ass along." Into view, half walking, half skipping, his lower lip caught between his teeth in mock shame, yet smiling and waving his hand, came one of the male models. He hurried past the group and into the motel office. Oliver stood back and let the door close after him.

"Oh, Mr. Bacon, what a morning! Not a cup of hot water! When I drew my bath every pore of my body was open like a flower, and—shiver my timbers, as we pirates say—it was cold as a stone! *Well,* I went to Derek's room. But that creature of his! There I stood in my bathrobe, unshaven, uncombed, unwashed, unhappy, looking like an old paper bag, and I asked that thing if I might kindly use her facilities. *Well,* she looked at me like a mute. Have you heard her *say* anything? I can understand the attraction of a quiet female, but he might as well have brought along a store dummy. Now, am I right or am I wrong, Mr. Bacon: our appearance is part of the photographer's responsibility, isn't it? Oh, I know I'm supposed to be the 'older male' in this epic. . . . You look surprised, Mr. Bacon? Should I take that as a compliment? I'm supposed to give a point of identification to your mature readership is the way I understand it. You do have older readers, don't you? Isn't that why that funny little man is editor? He *is* a funny little man. Probably not to you. But he has a funny little walk and a funny little mouth, and I find him quite nice. And right now you're saying to yourself, 'What kind of funny fellow is breaking bread with me?' aren't you, Mr. Bacon? But here I am, love me or leave me! *Well,* finally I shaved in cold water and cut off half my chinny-chin-chin. If it shows, well, we *are* supposed to board the ladies' boat by force. Oh, Lord, Look! There they go! Back to bed, everybody! How about you, Mr. Bacon, what are you going to do?"

Large drops of rain had begun falling fast and thick. The female models, hands over hair-dos, scattered toward their rooms. So did some of the men. Derek pulled his shirt over his cameras. Yoyo hunched over the equipment she carried and hurried to the office. The rest more or less followed her. As she came in, Arf could be heard shouting, "Stay dressed, girls! If it stops, we'll have to leave at a moment's notice."

The small office became crowded. Everyone had gotten quite wet in the few seconds' exposure. Mather, after wiping the water from his face and pulling his pants and shirt away from his skin, assumed a funeral director's stance—stomach out, somber, thoughtless. He avoided Oliver's eyes, and in turning his back to Oliver, Oliver could plainly see, outlined under the wet seat of his pants, a pancake-shaped object. Arf was last in and moved directly to the center of the group. "I want all the Christians among us to start praying to the patron saint of weather.

Oliver, who is the patron saint of weather? Saint Anthony?"

Oliver shrugged.

"Saint Anthony is lost objects," Derek said.

"He'll do. Because, my friends, the lost objects may be our jobs. There is five grand riding on this story, and if we return to New York with no more than happy memories of the fine food at Chez Mario and the wild nights at the Hampton Plaza, we'll be out on the street peddling dirty postcards. With that in mind, do I hear any suggestions?"

"Mr. Arf," Warren, the older model, said, "do you think we could have a *real* breakfast?"

"That's a good suggestion. Are there any other suggestions? Mother, perhaps you see some course of action."

Mather fingered his earlobe. "The best course of action —in answer to your question—in fact, the only course of action, as I see the situation, is simply to wait, but while waiting, continue our discussion. It's as simple as that."

"That's also a good suggestion. Derek?"

"I say let's get out on the boats and do the best we can. We can shoot the cabin shots. Then if it clears tomorrow, we can shoot the deck material."

"That's OK, Derek, except that we've paid fourteen hundred clams for one day's sailing only."

"And if it rains tomorrow?"

"That's it, my friend. Anyone else?"

Yoyo raised her hand like a schoolgirl and was acknowledged by a nod from Arf.

"I think," she said in a low voice, "that September is

a very sad month at the beach, but very beautiful too, especially in the rain. The light is so beautiful when it rains, but sad too. I think we should shoot a beach story with no people in it. All the crowds have gone home. There's a pail and shovel left by a child, beginning to rust. A lifeguard seat tipped over and half buried. An abandoned shack silvered by the weather. There actually is one about half a mile from here. Maybe we should have one girl walking along the shore, in the rain, all alone. . . ."

Arf was giving Derek a look of mock pity. Derek put a restraining hand on Yoyo's arm.

"Oliver, what do you have to say?"

Oliver shrugged.

"What have you got to say about this young lady's suggestion?"

He shrugged again.

"I agree. Now let me make a proposal. Here we are, at a motel. What are motels famous for? . . . OK, that being the case, they are even more so when it rains. 'What Do They Do at the Hampton Plaza Motel on a Rainy Afternoon?' . . . Dig?"

"What do they do, Mr. Arf?" Yoyo said.

"They fuck."

The girl looked blank.

"Isn't that what you would do, my child?"

"Leave her alone!" Derek said.

"It's a pleasure. All right, since there are no arguments, objections, counterproposals, let's get plotting."

The group went to Arf and Oliver's room; and it was

decided, mainly by Arf, that three bachelor girls would emerge from their room, ready for the beach, only to find it raining. At the same time, three bachelor boys would come out of their room next door. The boys invite the girls inside, and they begin to dance and drink. Two married couples, also in adjoining rooms, get together in the same way. The ten of them learn of one another's parties and form one large party, to be shot in Arf and Oliver's room.

Derek protested that there would not be enough space for ten characters.

"Baby," Arf said, "the closer they are, the better they look. That's the whole point. Three on one bed, boy-girl-boy. Three on the other, girl-boy-girl. Two on a chair. Two on the floor. Very orgy. The best we ever ran was the PTA shtick—nineteen parents and the teacher in one classroom."

"Please cast me on the bed," Warren said.

"What part do you want?"

"Boy-girl-boy."

"I repeat: what part do you want?"

"I'll leave that up to you, Mr. Arf."

"Anyway, children, I'd like to add a little Fellini touch. A fourth bachelor, a sadsack. We know he's a sadsack because we first see him dressed for the beach in his black shoes and brown socks. Not only is there no girl for him, but as everyone else gets undressed they hand him their clothes. By the end of the shtick he looks like a coat rack. Now who can play that part?" Arf looked around the room slowly. "Beryl, do you have any suggestions?"

"I couldn't play it," Beryl said.

"I should say not. We have better plans for you. No, we need . . . ah, Oliver! You!"

Oliver nodded without expression.

"No drama," Derek said.

"What?" Arf said.

"No drama, no movement, no suspense, no release."

"But plenty of advice. OK, let me think. . . . OK. The motel manager hears strange noises. He comes to investigate. He bursts into the room, ready to call the cops. But all five girls drop their partners, drag the old man onto the bed, and force him to participate."

"My dear Arf," Derek said, "is this to be a panel of twenty stills or a two-hour movie?"

"My dear Derek, you just shoot it, I'll edit."

"The man has delusions of Hollywood," Derek said.

"I have delusions of excellence."

"Who'll play the manager?" Derek asked.

"For that part I propose none other than our esteemed chief, the one man who can bring style and dignity to such a characterization—Ernest Mather. What do you say, Mother?"

Mather looked uncertain.

"All in good fun, Mother," Arf said, and there was a general murmur of agreement. "Everyone from publisher to copyboy will say that old Mother is a regular guy. He gave his all for Quiff. What do you say?"

There were more noises of assent, and Mather smiled nervously.

"You won't be sorry, Mother. All right, slaves, tell the

others to be here in ten minutes! We don't want it to stop raining."

The rain-discovery scenes were set up first. There was exposition trouble. How would the reader know the two parties were going on simultaneously? If the pictures cut back and forth between the bachelor party and the married party, wouldn't the reader be confused? Also, how would the reader know the married couples were married? Shots certainly couldn't be spent on close-ups of beringed fingers. After considerable discussion it was decided that everyone should emerge from four adjoining rooms at one time and immediately retire to Arf and Oliver's room for a single party.

Derek said that an overall rain-discovery shot would be ineffective because the figures would be too numerous and small. Nonetheless, one was taken, and everybody moved inside. Oliver had not brought a bathing suit. Arf decided this was fortuitous since he now had to pose in his undershorts, which would make him even more of a sadsack. Oliver removed his pants and shirt and took his place beside one of the beds.

When the shooting began, Arf started a running patter, some of which was specific suggestions: "You're not looking at the girl, you're watching someone else. If you want to play with the boy on the other bed, that's another shtick and another magazine," or, "She is not a twenty-buck hustler you can mount in ten seconds. This is a friendly gathering that might or might not get you somewhere. So take your hand off her ass and make like it's a seduction." And there were general comments to create an atmosphere: "Here we are, friendly, cozy. The whole day and maybe the whole night lies ahead of you. A little drink, a little talk, a touch here, a look there. Somebody laughs, somebody's sad. A gathering of young, attractive people enjoying. All the time in the world, all the flesh one could possibly want. We warm up slowly, boys and girls together. Sweet to be here. A kiss, a smile. Someone goes too far, someone else misses an opportunity. Like life, children. . . ."

After half an hour of various poses and arrangements, an hysterical gaiety had developed—giggling, pinching, mock and real outrage, an elbow in the eye, excuses, tears. It became impossible to control the actors. Finally Arf unscrewed a bulb from the floor lamp and dropped it onto the linoleum. It exploded, and everyone went still. "I'm sick of this shit," he said, "and if it goes on I'll see to it that your fees are cut in half. Your job is to shut up and stay put. You're fucking around, wasting my time and my patience, and I'm sick as shit of it. Do you understand? I want everyone to get dressed." Four of the five girls were bare-bosomed. The bikini top of one of the four hung loose around her neck. "We're going to start over. I have twenty rolls of nothing. You haven't communicated a story to me. You've just been fucking around. We should start with inhibition and decorum and end with abandon and licentiousness. You've been like kids in a playground throwing sand at one another. Now put those titties back and comb your hair!"

The two in the chair, a large blonde sitting on the copyboy's lap, giggled.

"What's funny?" Arf said.

"They're smoking pot," Derek said.

"For Christ's sake!" and with the side of his foot Arf kicked pieces of the broken bulb against the wall.

"Arf, Arf!" the copyboy said, making it sound like a bark.

"Get out!" Arf said, and turning to Derek, "We'll shoot without them."

The copyboy stood up, dumping the girl on the floor. In trying to help her up, he slipped himself. Some of the others picked them to their feet, and they left still giggling.

In five minutes everyone was dressed again. The girls had plucked their bikini tops from Oliver's dummylike outstretched hands. When one of them brushed her bare breasts against Oliver's arm for fun, two of the others did as well. Derek and Arf placed all of them at their posts and began shooting; but the frivolity, a little of which was necessary for lively pictures, was gone. Even the hawker's cadences had dropped from Arf's patter; he was reduced to concrete directions: "Raise your arm!" "Put your leg on his!" "Kiss his ear!" They shot another twenty rolls before moving on to the next part of the story, the arrival of the motel manager.

Arf prepared Mather with a public speech: "What are you, Mother? You run a motel. What does that tell us about you? It says that you are a bundle of contradictions. On the one hand, you're a personal servant. On the other, a capitalist. Some people come to your place for swimming and sun. All good and well. But, if that was all, you'd go broke. The profit is in the hot-pillow trade. You're ambivalent about them. They make you feel like a whore master. They also make you jealous. Night after night they do things you're not doing. It gets to you, it gets into your bones. In your deepest heart you hate them; but you have to keep smiling—right? This bunch, however, has gone too far. You hear wild noises, and in the morning yet! Squeals, laughter, suspicious silences, pounding feet, a portable phonograph blasting. You creep to the window, the shade is up, you peek in, and what do you see? At most you had expected three, four, maybe five people. But there are eleven. . . ."

"Nine," Derek said, "we dumped two."

"Nine people. Five fellas, four girls. This means eight titties and maybe one unmanly asshole. All your terrible ambivalences rise to the surface. They show in your face. What should you do? Blow the whistle? Call the cops? Or break in and confront these troublemakers? You're torn in half. Finally attraction overcomes repulsion; and you enter, finger raised like an avenging prophet. . . . Well, anyway, you get the picture. Now go outside and let's see that face in the window. . . . Pull up the blind, somebody!"

Derek knelt ten feet from the inside of the window, camera ready with a long lens. Arf squatted by his side. Mather appeared at the window, bent over, and brought his face close to the glass. He tried to produce the desired effect by cocking one eye and pulling down further the one usually drooping corner of his mouth. Everyone in the room watched him as if he were on stage. Derek began shooting, then stopped. "He looks like a madman," Derek said.

"Is it too much?"

"I don't know. Tell him to tone it down!"

Arf shouted so that Mather could hear outside. "Tone it down, Mother! You're not the phantom of the opera, you're just running a motel."

Mather stood up, worked his shoulders like an athlete loosening up, and applied his face to the window again.

"He still looks awful," Derek said, shooting rapidly. "Now he looks like a *corrupt* madman."

"Maybe it'll be good. Finish the roll, and we'll bring him in."

Arf got to his feet and went to the door. "OK, Mother, that was great. If we get canned from Quiff you can go into the movies."

"He can go into the circus," one of the female models said.

"Now I want you to come into the doorway, one hand on the knob and that index finger raised in warning. OK?"

Arf backed away to give Derek clearance. Derek had changed lenses and moved closer, still kneeling. Mather appeared in the doorway and assumed the position. He was half smiling now, apparently pleased with his own acting. "Wipe that smile off your face, Mother!" Arf said. Both corners of Mather's mouth turned down in what was intended to be a grimace. Oliver looked around the room. Everyone was transfixed.

Arf spoke quickly now. "One of you girls, someone

without a top, you, come up to him and take him by the
elbow! . . . That's it. Smile! . . . Guide him into the
room! . . . Another girl get on his other side! . . . Take
his other elbow! . . . Bring him in! . . . Farther! . . .
Farther! . . . That's it. . . . Near the bed! . . . OK. Girls,
sit down on the edge of the bed! . . . Pull him down between you! . . . Sitting! That's it. . . . For Christ's sake,
Mother, get that look off your face! You're supposed to
like this. The girls are getting through to you. A little
smile! Smile! You're grinning. No one's going to hurt
you. A nice little, natural smile. . . . Oh, Jesus! . . . OK.
Now, the girl on his right, lie back and pull him down
beside you! . . . That's it. Fall back, Mother! . . . Relax!
. . . That's it. Now the other girl, Lois baby, lie down on
the other side! You getting this, Derek? OK, now two
other girls, get onto the rest of the bed! Cover the bed
with flesh! . . . Ladies, you look like you're lying down
on the sidewalk. This is a bed. This is a seduction, not
a protest. Mother, move in on the bed more! Smile!
Look around you, look at the girls! . . . That's it. . . .
You're in heaven. You never had it so good. This is the
dream of a lifetime. . . . A dream, Mother, not a nightmare. . . . My God, this is *terrible*. . . . Girls, get up!
Mother, lie face down in the middle of the bed! Face
down! . . . That's it. Now, girls, one girl sit on each limb!
Spread your arms and legs, Mother! You won't hurt him,
girls. . . . That's it. Make out he's Christ and you're
crucifying him with your asses. Stop moving, Mother!
Stop! I said. Two of you guys, hold his legs! Hold his
arms! Get to it! Hold him! . . . Now two girls, get his

shirt off! Let's go! . . . More help! Hold him down! Every-body, hold him down! . . . Reach under and unbuckle the belt! . . . Now pull! OK, pull! Work it from top and bottom! . . ."

Near the end of the scene, there was so much noise in the room that Oliver couldn't hear what Mather was saying, but he was wriggling like a captured beast. The four men and women holding him were all necessary. Slowly the pants were worked over his buttocks. The un-dershorts came with them, and an object like a flattened icebag was revealed, apparently inserted in Mather's rectum. Oliver realized that this was Mather's way of dealing with his anxiety about soiling himself.

Oliver had maintained his sadsack pose and was the only one free to observe the motel manager looking in the window. The man had an inexpressive, weathered face, like a hard-working farmer's. A strong intuition told Oliver to get out. He dropped the models' bathing suits, took his shirt and pants from the bureau top, and slipped through the door. As far as he knew, no one saw him go. He dressed between two cars and walked through the rain to the East Hampton station, a mile away. There, soaking wet, he waited twenty minutes for the train.

Oliver unlocked the door of his apartment and pushed. It was chained from the inside and opened only three inches. Had he gone to the wrong door, which his key fit by chance? No, under his feet was his doormat, reading, WEL COME ON IN. Maybe the super's son had borrowed the super's keys and taken a girl in to screw. Or maybe it was burglars. Surprised burglars are dangerous. He could shout in through the crack and give them a chance to escape out the window. On the other hand they might shoot him through the door. He flattened himself against the wall and called, "Who's in there?"

"Oliver, is that you?"

It sounded like his mother. "Who's in there?"

"It's me, Oliver."

"Who's me?"

"Me!" A young female hand and wrist reached out, felt around, and withdrew. The door was then closed and the chain removed. The door opened wide. Cautiously Oliver looked around the door frame and saw Brooklyn, arms spread in welcome. She was dressed in his forest green pajamas. The pant legs were rolled up, the sleeves bunched up.

None of the girls had ever, ever used the house key without telling him beforehand. He gave a girl a key as a gesture, just as the girls had given him keys to their places as a gesture. This was a violation. To make it worse, Brooklyn was drunk. It was only the afternoon, and she was drunk. He'd never get rid of her. If he wasn't so wet and tired, he'd go to a movie. And if she was there when he got back he'd go to another movie, and then another, until she had gotten her ass *out*. But he was wet and tired.

"Oliver, you have the nicest bed in the world. Hmmm!" She put her hands, palms together, against her cheek. "Hmmm!" she said and rocked her torso from side to side.

He stepped into the foyer and removed his raincoat. The wet arms peeled off inside-out.

"Ollie-dollie, I shouldn't have busted in here, but something terrible happened to me."

He tried to loosen his tie, but its wet surfaces would not ride on one another. He yanked at it. The knot tightened into a small, hard mass. He lifted the half-undone tie over his head like a noose and dropped it at his feet. "Did somebody die?"

"My parrot."

"Your parrot died?"

"Yes."

"When did that happen?"

"Yesterday."

"Since when did you have a parrot?"

"I bought it two weeks ago."

He nodded and bent over to untie a shoe.

"I bought it when you left me."

He pulled off one wet sock. His foot was stained with dye.

"A parrot is supposed to live a hundred years," she said.

"That's probably an exaggeration."

"I'll say. It only lived two weeks. I bought it because I wanted something that would live longer than I would."

"How did it die?"

"It was asphyxiated."

"How did that happen?" He was down to his pants,

undershirt, and drawers. He decided to take his pants off but remove his underclothes in the bathroom. He unbuckled his belt and lifted one leg. In mimic unison she undid the pajama-bottom string and lifted one leg.

"The pilot light went off," she said.

He stepped out of the second leg and threw the pants on top of his other clothes on the floor. She did the same with her pajama bottoms. The top came down to her mid-thigh.

"I wouldn't have thought enough gas could come from a pilot light to kill a parrot," he said, facing her with his hands on his hips.

She faced him with her hands on her hips. "I called up the pet shop and when I told the man about the pilot light he said that was it."

"Maybe he sold you a sick bird and just said that."

"He said parrots are very sensitive to gas. They used them in the trenches in World War I to warn of gas attacks. If the parrot died, everyone had time to put on his gas mask. My grandfather was gassed in World War I."

"Sweetie, let's talk more about it in a little while. Can you amuse yourself while I take a shower?"

"I'm crying."

"I can see that."

"You don't care."

"I do, but I want to take a shower now."

"Can I come with you?"

"I just want to take a simple shower."

"I mean, come in the bathroom."

"If you want to. But then I'll have to get some sleep. I'm exhausted."

"All right, Oliver. But I have something very important to tell you. Do you want to have a little drink first?"

"Why should I want a little drink first?"

"I thought you might like one."

"What is it that you're going to tell me?"

"Go in the shower! In the shower I won't have to look at you."

"For Christ's sake, what is it?" False menses, the opposite of false pregnancy?

"Go in the shower!"

He thought of gas chambers, but he went into the bathroom and stepped into the bathtub, which doubled as a shower. He pulled the curtain, took off his undershirt and drawers, checked the drawers for stains, and draped both on the shower curtain rod. He looked over the rod. Brooklyn had seated herself with drunken straightness on the open toilet. "What do you want to tell me?"

"Turn the water on!"

"I won't be able to hear you."

"I don't want you to hear me. I have to make peepee."

"For Christ's sake!"

"Please, Oliver, be a gentleman!"

He pointed the shower nozzle down and turned on the water. It splattered at his feet. After about thirty seconds he turned it off. "Did you go?"

"No. You embarrassed me."

"Do you want me to turn the water on again?"

"No, it doesn't matter."

"Are you going to tell me what it is you wanted to tell me?"

"First I want to tell you how I came to be here."

"That's not the special thing, though."

"I'll get to that."

"Why don't you tell me that first. I feel stupid standing in here."

"Would you rather take the shower and then I tell you?"

"Why don't you tell me now, then I'll take the shower, then you can tell me how you came to be here?"

"I found it dead when I got home from the office last night. . . ."

"Is that the special thing?"

"It's all *connected*, Oliver."

"OK."

"I was going to call it Felix or Felicia, depending on its sex. The man sold it to me without telling me the sex, and I forgot to ask. So I called the pet shop, even though it was dead, and then I called you. But no one was home."

"I was out on the Island for the magazine."

"I thought it was something like that, because I called you till two A.M., and then I came over. I put the chain on the door in case you came back with somebody. You're not angry with me, are you, Oliver? I couldn't stay alone with him."

"Him?"

"Felix. The man told me it was a male, so I named it posthumously."

"But that's not the special thing, is it?"

"No, it's that I'm not on the side of life anymore."

"*What?*"

"You left me because I was on the side of life, didn't you?"

"What are you talking about?"

"Because I wanted to *bear* life—that was why you left me, wasn't it?"

"Look, first I had that prostrate trouble, and then everything was getting too mixed up to cope with. I needed to be alone for a while."

"Just the opposite of me, Oliver. Maybe that's why we were attracted to one another. It's ironic. Anyway, I've looked my character in the eye and I'm not on the side of life anymore. I'm on the side of death. I bought a new diaphragm."

Oliver said nothing.

"I did."

"OK."

"But you don't want me under any circumstances, do you?"

"Sweetie, let me take this shower, and then I'll come out and explain how I feel."

"I know already."

"I doubt it. But I'm going to take this shower now. You go out and fix yourself a nice little drink, OK?" He turned on both handles, put his head into the rush of water, and adjusted the temperature to a comfortable

119

hot. After the chill wet of his clothes on the station plat-
form and their sweaty wet on the train into the city, the
steady flow of water was a treat. He decided to stay under for a long time. It would give her a chance to have
another drink, maybe even get dressed and leave. As the
water beat on his scalp and shoulders and ran over his
face he hummed, "I'm gonna wash that girl right out of
my hair." He soaped his pubic hair and repeated the
line. Then he remembered the message of the song and
sang it to himself. After he was thoroughly washed and
warmed, he decided to look over the curtain and see if
she was still there. He felt under control, although a
certain tingle did play near the base of his spine. Would
she be bent over to pick up a hairpin? She had such a
sweet ass! Would this be the end of his experiment? He
knew how desire, any kind of desire, could compromise
resolutions by making the mind produce larger resolutions that had room for one little exception. He looked.
She was still there, on the toilet, her legs spread now,
elbows on knees, face in hands, eyes closed. She was
straining at her stools. He returned to the shower spray
and waited for the flush, again saved by happenstance.

An hour later they were sitting in the living room,
she on the couch with her feet tucked under her, he
slumped in a stuffed chair. She had put the pajama bottom
back on, but its large fly was open. He had dressed himself
in clean slacks and a tennis shirt. They were both drinking
bourbon, she faster than he. She seemed to have hit her

second wind, and although her eyes had turned watery she talked coherently. At least he thought so. He was so tired—and now he was getting drunk again—that he could not attend closely. As far as he could tell, she was worried that death was not going to wait for August any more but was going to visit every month. "Why else did Felix die in September?" she would ask. Sometimes he said he didn't know, sometimes he said because the pilot light went out. He would have gone to bed except that he was sure she would get in with him and that that would be the end. He half hoped that he would fall asleep in the chair. Then, when he awoke, maybe she would be gone.

Suddenly the buzzer from the downstairs bell rang.

"Leave it!" he said.

"Who is it, Oliver?"

"Someone is trying to get in downstairs."

They heard the buzzer ring in another apartment. "See," he said.

Soon, however, the upstairs bell rang. Oliver held up his hand. "Nobody I know would come here without telephoning."

It rang again, more insistently.

"It's a salesman," he said.

"It's a telegram," she said.

It rang again. Then came a deep, clear voice, "I know you're in there, Bacon."

"Who is that?" Oliver whispered.

"I know she's in there too," the voice said.

"Do you know who it is?" Oliver said to Brooklyn.

"I don't, Oliver. I swear I don't."

"Well, then the hell with them."

"Open this goddamned door, Bacon!"

Oliver went to the foyer. "Who's out there?"

"Open the goddamned door! This is Gus Bauer. I know Lillian is in there."

"Gus Bauer!"

"Open up, or, so help me, God, I'll break the door down."

"Gus, I'm going to call the police unless you get your ass away from my door *immediately*."

"You do that, Bacon, and when I tell them my wife's in there, *they'll* break the door down."

"Gus, I give you my word of honor. . . ."

"Your word of *what?*"

They were both silent.

"I saw her in there."

"She's not here, Gus."

"I've been watching you both from the roof across the street."

"It's another woman, Gus."

"If it's not Lillian, why don't you open the door?"

"You're in a funny mood out there. I don't *want* to open the door."

Silence.

"What made you come here in the first place?"

"She wasn't in her bed this morning. Where else would she go?"

"There are plenty of places she could have gone, Gus."

"Are you saying she's having other affairs?"

"No, Gus. But she could have gone to her mother's."

"Her mother's dead, and her father lives in California."

"She could be in a hotel."

"Do you know how I *know* she's in there?"

"How?"

"The key you gave her was gone."

Silence.

"Listen, Gus, if I get the woman who is in here to say something through the door, will that convince you?"

Silence.

"Yes."

"OK. Hold on!"

But Brooklyn lay unconscious on the couch. Her drink had spilled onto the floor. Oliver tried to revive her until, finally, the bell rang again.

Oliver hurried back to the foyer. "Gus, listen, this is God's honest truth. The girl in here has passed out. . . . How much did you see from the roof? Could you see that she was drinking?"

"God damn you, Bacon! I'll break this door down. Then I'll break your neck and hers too."

"Gus, wait a minute! I'll put the chain on the door. I'll bring her out here and you can *see* her. OK?"

". . . OK."

Oliver chained the door and opened it.

Brooklyn was completely slack. He put his hands under her arms from the front, but the arms went up over her head when he tried to lift her. He picked her up like a child, but the head hung back in a frightening way. He returned her to the couch and fitted his hands under her arms from behind, then walked her backwards so that her heels dragged along the rug. He had to watch where he was going, so not until he was about to come into view from the doorway did he see that her pajama bottoms had come off. He laid her down on the rug, retrieved the pajamas and fitted them on, one leg at a time. He couldn't help but come face to face with her pubic area, and the sweetness of the female genital almost overcame him. For an instant he thought of having noisy intercourse with her there on the floor while Gus listened from the hall. Instead he dragged her into the foyer.

"Satisfied?"

"I can't see her."

"Which part do you want to see, Gus?"

"Her face."

"I don't want you to see her face."

"Is she a movie star or something?"

"You can see her hand, that's enough."

Brooklyn stirred and vomited on her chest.

"All right, satisfied? Now fuck off!"

In a few seconds, Oliver heard descending footsteps on the stairs. Brooklyn became half conscious. He sat her up on the floor and got wet towels from the bathroom. As he cleaned her she alternately retched and said she was sorry. Eventually she was clean enough to be taken to his bed. Then under a quilt he went to sleep on the couch.

There he dreamed he was walking naked, his erect penis wagging in front of him, through a sunny field of glass tubes about a foot high and of a familiar width. They were strangely interesting, and just as he realized that they were intended for intercourse, he noticed that beside each tube was a sign like the signs identifying plants in a botanical garden. He bent over to read one. It said, FUCK ME. He read others; they all expressed the same sense in different words: HUMP ME, BANG ME, STICK ME, PUMP ME, BOUNCE ME, JUMP ME. There were perhaps a thousand tubes in the field. If each one, as seemed to be the case, had a sign like these, they would add up to an important linguistic contribution. Nowhere that he knew were there a thousand synonyms for fucking. Unfortunately, as he wandered about, reading new signs, he found he was forgetting those he had just read. Without paper and pencil the words would be lost. Suddenly he came to one sign that seemed particularly eloquent. LOVE ME, it said; but its tube seemed like all the others. "I'm very excited," he said aloud, as if to assure the tubes that at least one of them would be favored. "Which one will it be?" he also said, thinking this would tantalize the tubes. "Will it be you?" he said to one tube and bent over to read its sign. It said, PRICK ME. This struck him as ambiguous and made him doubt the tube's goodwill. Then he realized that any one of these tubes, regardless of its sign, might, if he chose it, break off around his penis. He didn't believe it would cut him, but it certainly was possible that a jagged ring of glass could remain on his penis and injure any real woman he had intercourse with in the future. He felt fortunate and virtuous that he had discovered this evil possibility in time; and, as if in reward, a real woman, very round and buxom, like no woman he had ever had intercourse with, beckoned from the edge of the field. "Coming," he called and hurried through the field dodging tubes like a football runner. As he approached her she smiled and stepped lithely back into a heavy woods, not to escape him but to find a secluded and comfortable place for them. As he closed the space between her and himself the air became pleasantly damp and the woods darker. He reached her and the desired place at the same time. He took her into his arms, and they fell into a deep pile of wet leaves the green of faded money. As they sank down, he ejaculated. Had he entered her? He wasn't sure. He reached into the leaves to feel the outline of her body. She had disappeared. "Well, better than a tube," he said; and the dream ended.

Oliver woke at dawn Sunday. He slipped his hand under the front of his slacks to see if his underwear was damp, and it was. He hadn't had a wet dream in years. If the mind were to produce a wet dream every night, he considered, there would be no need for waking sex. But then the race would die out. Suddenly he recognized the beckoning woman from the dream as a character in Quiff's nymph-satyr cartoons. Anyone like her in real life would be repulsive; his pleasure in recollecting the dream was gone. Brooklyn and the details of the previous day came back to him. He threw off the quilt and sat up on the couch. Outside, a steady drizzle fell. He pictured Arf and Mather on Long Island and was pleased at the thought of their discomfort. When he stood up he felt tipsy and bloated. Was Brooklyn gone? If she was, he could get back into bed with the newspaper and stay there till afternoon. Oh, let her be gone! Because if she wasn't, he would have to stay up and talk. They would start drinking again, and he'd be out of shape till Tuesday or even Wednesday. Quietly he went to the bedroom. The bed was made. He explored the rest of the apartment. Except for a letter on the kitchen table, there were no signs even of her having been there. In a large hand the letter filled six pages. He decided to read it over breakfast. From the hall he brought the Times to read after the note and set about fixing eggs and bacon.

"Oliver," the note began. The absence of a "Dear" meant something unpleasant was coming, so he decided to look at the newspaper with breakfast and read the letter afterward. In the garden section he found an interesting article on growing plants under artificial light. Then, over coffee, he turned to the letter.

"Oliver,

"It is dead of night. I certainly hope you do not wake up before I finish this. If you wake up now I won't be able to face you. I am about to tell you something that will shock you. Also, I am about to break two promises, one to myself and one to another. I refer to Lillian Bauer. Yes, Lillian Bauer. Does that surprise you? Did you ever think I would be making and breaking a promise to Lillian Bauer? Nor did I. I sit here in the dead of night, knowing you are only yards away, immersed in your dreams. I, too, am immersed in dreams, but they are more like nightmares, I can tell you. Perhaps I am wrong in revealing this to you, perhaps right. Time will tell. Well, Lillian Bauer's husband was not far wrong yesterday! Lillian was here in this apartment! She left only minutes before you arrived! Oh, what a tangled web we weave when first we practice to deceive, Oliver! Like myself, she needed you Friday night, and I am not talking about what you think—we were both clear on that. I am not even talking about love. I am talking about friendship —yes, friendship—which at times you are capable of giving a unique kind of to others. This is your great gift, Oliver, and I tell you this not to swell your ego, because your ego needs no swelling from me, God knows, but because it is the simple truth. Back to Lillian. She was unable to sleep, unable even to remain at her husband's side. Thus she rose from her bed and drove from Long Island, arriving here at 9 A.M. I was asleep for six or seven hours at the time. With a key she opened the door which was chained by me. (How many keys have you passed out, Oliver? Five, ten, a hundred? And what must one do to be a member of your key club? Oh, really! Is it as simple as that?) She unlocked the door and found it, as I said, chained. She was sure you were inside, but she did not know whether you were alone or not. If it turned out that you were with someone else, she decided to use the pain she would experience to end her feelings for you forever. So she rang the bell! I must have been deeply immersed in sleep, because she rang for many minutes before I woke up. I was sure it was you, and seeing Lillian made no difference. You were just bringing home another member of your key club. Even when I opened the door all the way, I thought you were standing behind her or running down the stairs in embarrassment. What followed was a very ticklish confrontation, I can tell you. Lillian, too, thought, *you* were standing behind *me!* So she said that although she had come to see you, she didn't want to anymore and was sorry for waking us. I could plainly see what she was going through, and after explaining the situation to her I pointed out that obviously we had many things in common and she should come in so we could talk. For a long time she did not tell me her name. I did not ask her and she did not tell me. What she did was to mention Lillian Bauer as if it was another person. She told me how a jealous girlfriend of yours had phoned this Lillian Bauer and threatened to reveal her affair. Was I that girl, she wanted to know. I assured her that I was not and no amount of jealousy could ever force me to commit such a cruel and insane act. Then she said that *she* made the phone call to Lillian Bauer and had been lying to me to see what I thought of it! This mystified me completely, as you might well imagine. Finally it dawned on me that *she* must be Lillian Bauer. So I accused her point-blank. You are Lillian Bauer, I said. Well, she broke down and admitted it. It was at this point that we decided to drown our sorrows, so to speak, which I tell you so that you will not think the condition you found me in was arrived at by myself. The mutual unburdening that followed has been a great help to both of us, I believe. Lillian said that she now feels you are still a little boy and not capable of taking on the burdens of a family. When I told her about your fright at the

thought of my conceiving a child, even though I offered
to bring it up myself, she asked how she could have been
so foolish as to think you were capable of taking care of
a whole family such as hers. Then she said—and I tell
you this with both laughter and the bitter taste of ashes
in my mouth—that she was bowing out in favor of me.
She said she thought I was the one for you. I laugh now
because I, too, am bowing out—in favor of whom? Not
the monster of the phone call, I hope. When Lillian left
she was crying and feeling no pain, as they say. It was
then that she asked me not to tell you she had been here.
I solemnly promised I wouldn't. That promise is now
broken. Why am I breaking it? Because I want you to
understand, Oliver, how terrible is your power over
others. I left the towel and pajamas in the bathtub."

He folded the letter, uncertain what to do with it. Ever
since Florida had discovered his sex records he was wary
of keeping personal papers around. Still, this was a doc-
ument of sorts. He might work it into a Quiff feature.
"Strange Love Letters I Have Received." By an anonymous cocksman. Oliver once had a long letter from Long
Island about Gus' premature ejaculations; but he tore
it up without finishing it, feeling at the time that there
were limits to infidelity.

After reading over the rest of the newspaper he tried
to compose a letter supposedly from the mother of a
young girl the anonymous cocksman was screwing. The
mother threatens a statutory rape charge unless . . . unless he shares the cock with *her*. But it didn't at all
go well. The mother's invitation had to be implied
rather than stated, and the subtle demands of innuendo

were beyond him in his present mood. After sitting immobile at his typewriter for twenty minutes, he glanced at the electric clock and saw that it was 9:13. An idea occurred to him so good that he felt it as a flash in his head. It was Sunday, true, but even if Gus answered it he could handle it. At exactly 9:15 he rang Long Island's number. Gus answered.

"Gus?"

"Yes?"

"This is Oliver Bacon."

Silence.

"You there, Gus?"

"Yes."

"Gus, excuse me for calling, but I was worried about Lillian. Did she get home OK?"

"Yes."

"And she's OK?"

"Yes."

"That's all I wanted to know actually. I didn't want to talk to her particularly. But, Gus, may I ask you something? Did you tell her you were in town looking for her?"

"No."

"That's all I wanted to know, Gus, and that she got home OK. Great, Gus. Thanks."

Oliver waited, and when the line stayed open he hung up.

He considered calling Florida, but then he thought it better to let sleeping dogs lie. Also, Florida had never really complained about her husband.

Ten minutes later, Long Island called back.

"Oliver, did you call here a little while ago?"

"Yes. Did he tell you?"

"No. But he stood there with a dead phone in his hand for five minutes and just stared at me. Why did you do it, Oliver?"

"I wanted to talk to you."

"Oliver, it's *Sunday*."

"I know. I'm sorry. Where is he now?"

"He went out for a walk."

"In the rain?"

"In the rain. What did you say to him?"

"I asked how you were."

"Oliver, are you crazy?"

"I'm sorry."

"Well, it's too late now. What do you really want?"

"I just want to talk to you."

"On *Sunday?*"

"I'm sorry."

"All right. I'm here now. Talk!"

"Isn't this call going to be listed on your bill?"

"Oliver, things can't get any worse. That I called you, at this point it doesn't matter."

"I thought things were going better."

"What makes you think that? You have no way of knowing how things are going. You haven't called me once."

"I'm sorry. Are thing *not* going well?"

"Terrible."

"Gee, that's awful. . . . I've been thinking a lot about you and Gus lately."

"Thinking what?"

"Well, say, if I were an analyst and I asked you to put in a nutshell what was wrong with Gus, what would you say?"

"I'd say. . . ."

"Let me get a cigarette, sweetie. Hold on!" Oliver brought paper and pencil to the phone table. "Yes, you'd say. . . ."

"I'd say in a nutshell that he is not sensitive, not . . . finely tuned."

"Not finely tuned."

"In a nutshell, that's what I'd say."

"How do you mean, not finely tuned?"

"Insensitive."

"In what way?"

"In a lot of ways, Oliver. I could make a list of the tiny little things that separately wouldn't mean a thing, but together they just add up to . . . insensitivity."

"You told me how lousy bed was."

"If that was all, I could cope with it; but it's *every-thing.*"

"You could cope with bed, if everything else was all right?"

"I think so."

"Does it ever work?"

"Bed?"

"Yes."

"I told you about that."

"About the premature ejaculations, you mean."

"Even that isn't the worst."

"What's worse?" In turning a page, Oliver dropped the notebook. "Hold on a second, I dropped something. . . . Yes, that's not the worst. What's worse?"

"It makes me queasy even to talk about it."

"Gee, don't if it makes you queasy."

"It's not that I'm squeamish, it's just that it's another one of those stupid little things *I cannot stand!*"

"I doesn't sound like a stupid little thing."

"It's not. To *me!* . . . . Oliver, he breaks wind in bed."

"No kidding. How do you mean? On purpose?"

"When he's asleep."

"I didn't know people could do it in their sleep."

"He does."

"Jesus, that really stinks. I mean, added to everything else."

"It is *the* most disgusting thing in the world."

"I'll bet."

"I have a system, though."

"A system?"

"I open the covers at the bottom of the bed. . . ."

"Yes."

". . . and I open them on Gus' side. . . ."

"Yes."

". . . and then I sleep with my arms on top of the blankets pressing down."

"So it doesn't get at you."

"Exactly. Sometimes it does, though. Sometimes I fall asleep and move my arms up. Or if it's cold I have to keep them under the covers. In that case, I try to tuck the blankets in around my neck, sort of under my shoulders."

"Does it ever wake you up?"

"Sometimes. Although usually if I'm asleep I stay asleep. I have been awakened, though."

"By the noise or the thing itself?"

"It's hard to tell. When you're awakened like that, you can't always tell what it was that woke you up. . . . Oliver, I think he's coming. I have to go. Call me, Oliver!"

Using Long Island's information as a start, Oliver spent the afternoon inventing a memoir by a wife whose husband had Gus' trouble. She tried separate beds, but the husband could not sleep alone. They consulted their doctor, and he prescribed bland food, a long walk in the evening, and a thorough bowel movement before retiring —to no avail. Then one evening at a party the wife chanced to tell her problem to a chemist. The chemist said there must be many such sufferers in the world and promised to try to do something about it. The next day he purchased a surplus army gas mask and with the filter made a device to go over the rectal aperture. No luck. The farts remained offensive. The chemist then tried the filtering substances from various cigarettes. The old Columbia-Strickland filter worked well on the initial fart but broke down thereafter; the others were no use at all. One day it occurred to the chemist that probably farts, being a natural gas, were combustible. He was troubled with flatulence himself; so he dropped his pants, crouched over a mirror he had placed on the floor, and passed a lighted match under his ass, farting as he did. There was an unmistakable and rather attractive blue flash and no odor at all. The chemist was jubilant, because the rest was merely a matter of mechanics—the creation of an unobtrusive device that would act as a pilot light at the vestibule of the rectal passage. A patent, the wife reports, is now pending; and, as soon as the chemist has perfected a silencer for the mechanism, he intends to market it. Oliver entitled the article "Gusts" in honor of Gus Bauer and after supper took the phone off the hook so he could spend an undisturbed evening polishing it. He had recently heard that the publisher wanted more humor in Quiff.

As soon as Oliver walked into the office on Monday morning, Mather's secretary hurried over and told him the publisher wanted to see him.

"What about?"

"I don't know, Mr. Bacon."

"Where's Mother?"

"He's not in yet, Mr. Bacon."

"When he comes in, tell him where I am, will you?"

"Yes, sir."

"That ought to wake him up."

She smiled cautiously, as always when possibly derisive remarks were made about the boss.

The organization put out fourteen magazines with the help of two hundred editors. Rumors of promotions, shifts, retirements, firings were always in the air. The latest concerned the editor of Technics Today, Lester Cushman. It looked like he was headed up from editorial to general administration, and since the assistant editor of Technics Today had body odor a replacement would probably come from elsewhere in the organization. A year or so before, on a free-lance basis, Oliver had written a piece for the magazine called "Pullout to Pill: Man's Frustrating Attempts to Frustrate Conception," which had been well received. Perhaps the publisher remembered it and now wanted to offer him Lester Cushman's job. The idea didn't appeal to Oliver, but he thought he should be prepared to reject it gracefully, so he sat down at his desk and called Lester.

After asking about the wife and kids and remarking that it had been too long between lunches, Oliver said, "I've been hearing things. . . . No, about *you*. . . . That you're headed upstairs. . . . Who? Actually *who?* . . . From Lou Prepobotzo. In Promotion. . . . *He* knows *you*. . . . Just that you were headed upstairs. . . . No, nothing definite. . . . I see. . . . Anyway, it looks pretty good there, baby. Rumors and everything. . . . No, nothing else. . . . You bet I will. . . . Sure, even rumors. . . . Right. . . . Right. . . . Immediately. . . . You bet. . . . Lester, they're calling me. . . . You bet. Soon." Oliver put down the phone, sighed, and said, "Poor slob."

The publisher's office, known as the Old Man's hole, was on the twenty-second and top floor. Oliver had been there once before—had, in employee parlance, "penetrated the Old Man's hole." The occasion had been a

Publisher's Prize for conducting a symposium among well-known American males about how much and what kind of body hair they preferred on women. George Plimpton had liked "a normal amount in the usual places." John Simon admitted to "a taste for a modicum of facial hair." Seymour Krim enjoyed "flowing head hair, definitely hair under the arms, a kinky bush, and one curly devil on the titty tip." Joe Namath "never thought about it." The feature had won the prize, not because it had appealed to the publisher particularly, but because it had generated so much comment in the women's magazines.

Now the assurance with which the publisher's secretary recognized his name and sped him into the publisher's office set Oliver's sweat glands tingling. The publisher was not the old man of his title, but plump, blond, and middle-aged, with a perpetual tan. He was seated behind his large desk at the far end of the long room. He did not rise, as he had at the award, but nodded Oliver into the visitor's chair. They studied one another. The publisher spoke first: "I'd like you to tell me your view of it. I want you to take your time and think about what you say before you say it. I also want you to think about what you don't say before you fail to say it."

"I'm Oliver Bacon, sir."

"Yes."

"I mean, don't you have the wrong man, sir?"

"You're the assistant editor of Quiff?"

"Yes, sir."

"And you have no more to tell me than your name?"

"I have a number of things I'd like to *discuss* with you, sir."

"Go on!"

"Well, for one thing, sir, as I understand it, you feel we need more humor in Quiff. . . ."

The publisher held up his hand. "You returned to the city Saturday afternoon, is that right?"

"From Long Island? Yes, sir."

"Why?"

"This is where I live, sir."

"I want to know why you left the Hampton Plaza Motel."

"Oh, you want to know why I left the Hampton Plaza Motel."

The publisher nodded.

"I wanted to get away from it, sir."

"Yes, that sounds reasonable. Why did you want to get away from it?"

"I wanted to get away from it, sir," Oliver said, rolling his right hand as if winding wool, "because of the atmosphere."

"What was the atmosphere?"

"You really would have to have been there to understand it, sir."

"I wasn't there but I'm trying to understand it."

"I don't know if I can explain it, sir."

"Try!"

"I am trying, sir."

"I don't think you are, Mr. Bacon."

"I really am, sir."

"Try harder!"

"Would it be easier if you told me what we're getting at, sir?"

"No."

"I see. Well, I gather, sir, something has happened."

"Do you know what happened?"

"No, sir."

"Have you had any phone calls from East Hampton?"

"No, sir."

"No calls from the East Hampton police?"

"No, sir."

"How would you like to play a little game with me, Mr. Bacon?"

"Sure, sir."

"An editor like yourself is supposed to have imagination, is that right?"

"Yes, sir. If you remember, you commended me on my imagination when you gave me the Publisher's Prize for the symposium on women's body hair."

"Yes, well, I'm thinking of a different kind of imagination, *historical imagination.*"

"I see, sir."

"What I'd like you to do is to imagine for me what happened at the Hampton Plaza Motel after you left Saturday."

"I see, sir."

"Do you have historical imagination, Mr. Bacon?"

"I may have, sir."

"Shall we see if you do?"

Oliver cleared his throat. "May I have a moment to think, sir?"

The publisher nodded.

"Well, sir, I assumed from the fact that we're here talking that something dramatic happened."

The publisher nodded.

"And I imagine that the dramatic thing that happened was of a pretty serious nature."

"Mr. Bacon, you're analyzing. I asked you to imagine. I want you to let your imagination *run riot*."

"May I ask you something, sir?"

The publisher nodded.

"Why do you want me to do this, sir?"

"Let's say that I want to see what you're made of, Mr. Bacon."

"Aren't there better ways of accomplishing that, sir?"

"No."

"I see. Sir, do you actually know what happened after I left?"

"Just tell me what *you* think happened, not what you think *I* think happened."

Oliver took a deep breath. "Well, sir, when I left. . . ."

"Yes."

"I'll assume, sir, that you know what happened before I left. Shall I do that?"

"Yes."

"Mr. Mather, who had his pants off, sir, broke loose from the models who were holding him and hid under the bed. . . ."

"Yes."

"Well, Mr. Arf, who wanted to finish the story we were shooting—we were shooting a pixshtick about an orgy in a motel room on a rainy day, sir—Mr. Arf had to get Mr. Mather out from under the bed. He pleaded with him, but that didn't work. He threatened him, but that didn't work either. Then he tried to poke Mr. Mather out with a broom, but Mr. Mather got hold of the broom and pulled it under the bed with him. . . . Are you following me, sir?"

The publisher nodded.

"Well, then Mr. Arf and the male models thought they could move the bed from over Mr. Mather. But that didn't work either. Mr. Mather just scrambled under wherever they moved the bed to. Well, one of the male models, named Warren, said he would get under the bed *with* Mr. Mather and coax him out. Well, that was a mistake, because Mr. Mather bit him on the chest, around the nipple. Warren came out screaming and crying—he was actually bleeding—and ran into the bathroom. Then a really frightening thing happened. Mr. Mather started to growl like a dog and bark. . . ."

"What were the others doing at this time?"

"I was getting to that, sir. Two of the female models began making love to one another, and this sort of drew the attention away from Mr. Mather. That was going along fine, until one of the male models—not Warren—decided he would try to make love to one of the female models making love to the other female model. Well, all hell broke loose. The two female models attacked the male model and would have seriously injured him if still another male model hadn't intervened. . . ."

"What was Mr. Arf doing at this point?"

"Well, that's a story in itself. Mr. Arf was very upset and accidentally broke one of the cameras of the photographer, Derek. Derek was furious. The camera was on a leather strap, and Derek swung it around and hit Mr. Arf in the mouth with it, breaking three of his teeth. Blood came pouring out of Mr. Arf's mouth, and he ran into the bathroom with Warren, and before anyone knew about it the door was locked. Meanwhile the two male models—the one who had been attacked by the female models and the other one who tried to save him. . . ."

"I get the picture, Mr. Bacon."

"I'm not finished, sir."

"All right, go on!"

"The only sane one there. . . ."

"Since you yourself were gone."

"Right! The only sane one there was Derek's assistant, a little blond girl named Yoyo. She wanted to get a pail of water to pour on the two female models, and on the two male models, who now were also making love to one another. But the bathroom door was locked. So, what did she do? She found some bottles of whiskey and emptied *them* on the embracing couples. Well, you can imagine what the place looked and smelled like when the East Hampton police arrived."

"I don't know if I can, Mr. Bacon."

"Well, Warren and Mr. Arf were given first aid, and Mr. Mather was taken to the hospital, where he's being tested for rabies. . . . That's all, sir . . . Was I close?"

"I hope not, Mr. Bacon. As you suggested, Mr. Mather is in the East Hampton Memorial Hospital. The others,

I believe, are in jail, with the exception of your copyboy and a woman named Gloria Candlemaker."

"They're in *jail*, sir?"

"That would seem to be the logical consequence of the scene you described."

"But I was just making it up, sir. What are they in jail *for?*"

"No one has been formally charged, but I understand that the possibilities include possession of drugs, contributing to the delinquency of a minor. . . ."

"Who's that, sir?"

"One of the girls is seventeen."

"That isn't the photographer's assistant, is it, sir?"

"I don't know. But what makes the situation rather serious is that Chief Vollhaus has a photographic record of the debacle—fourteen hundred color transparencies. Among other things, they show, as you suggested, sexual perversion."

"What kind, sir?"

"Chief Vollhaus claims that there are pictures of one of the party—Mr. Mather, I gather—using an 'autoerotic anal device.' Can you clarify that, Mr. Bacon?"

"That was when I left, sir."

"I understand that you were in a number of the pictures yourself, but not taking part. You were the one in undershorts?"

"Yes, sir."

"What about this anal erotic device?"

"Actually, sir, it was sort of a thing inserted in Mr. Mather's rectum."

"I see. Well, the pictures will tell us more about that. General Counsel has flown out to talk with Chief Vollhaus. If the chief is to be believed, no reporters know about the affair. I talked with the copyboy last night. He and this girl seem to have been fed up with the goings-on too. I called you a number of times, but your phone was busy."

"I took it off the hook, sir, to work on a piece for the magazine. I'm tentatively calling it 'Gusts'. . . ."

The publisher held up his hand. "You had no inkling that we were in danger of a damaging scandal?"

"None whatsoever, sir."

"I also talked by phone with Mr. Arf."

"How is he, sir?"

"Angry."

"Angry, sir?"

"He claims you called the police."

"That's not true, sir."

"That's what he claims."

"Has he proof, sir?"

"I gather he put two and two together and decided that, since the police arrived shortly after you left, you called them."

"That's not the case, sir. The motel manager was looking in the window. It was probably the motel manager who called."

"Yes, well Chief Vollhaus says that the initiating call came from a man who claimed to be the manager. I have also talked with him, and he claims he did not make the call. So you can see, it's quite complicated."

"It certainly is, sir. But I didn't make the call."

"Yes, well, let's see what happens. I have a feeling that Chief Vollhaus can be persuaded to release the group and turn over the pictures."

"You mean by bribery, sir?"

"We don't bribe people, Mr. Bacon. We compensate them for their trouble."

"I see, sir."

"We will also compensate the motel manager for his trouble."

"There's the answer, sir. That's why he denied making the call. If he had admitted it, there'd be no money in it for him."

"That's possible. The point is that now it doesn't matter who made the call."

"It matters to me, sir."

"But you know who made the call, Mr. Bacon."

"I do *not*. All I know is that *I* didn't make it."

"Then why does it concern you?"

"It concerns me that other people think I did. Do *you?*"

"That's not important now."

"It *is* important." Oliver stood up, it seemed to him, involuntarily.

"What happened at East Hampton is in the hands of General Counsel. What is important to you, Mr. Bacon, is Quiff. I don't think Mr. Mather can come back to the magazine."

"Where will he go?"

"Let's not discuss Mr. Mather. Let's discuss you, Mr.

Bacon. Under ordinary circumstances you would be next in line for the job. You understand that."

The publisher waited, Oliver said nothing, and the publisher went on. "How do you feel about that?"

"I don't know, sir."

"Well, why don't you sit down and decide how you feel about it?"

Oliver sat down. The publisher waited again. "I don't want you to think in silence, Mr. Bacon. That doesn't help me at all."

"I don't know what I think yet."

"Let me help you. Do you want the job?"

"That's what I don't know, sir."

"Do you think you can do the job?"

"Yes, sir."

"Why?"

"I practically do it now."

"I see. What you're saying is that Mr. Mather has let his subordinates run the magazine."

". . . Not exactly."

"What are you saying then?"

Silence.

"For some reason, this is a difficult area for you, Mr. Bacon. But don't make it difficult for me! I have to find a successor to Mr. Mather. Are you or are you not interested?"

". . . I'm interested."

"Good. You're interested, and I'm interested. Now tell me more about your connection with this affair!"

"Well, sir, what can I say? I wasn't keen on it. To put it mildly."

"Why was that?"

"For one thing, it was too expensive."

"What was the budget?"

"Five thousand, I believe, sir." The publisher's eyes narrowed, and Oliver went on. "Do you know how the thing got started? I mean, to shoot the original story on the bay?"

"Why don't you tell me all about it. . . . Wait!" The publisher told his secretary through the intercom not to interrupt them. Then he offered Oliver a cigar, which Oliver accepted. The publisher leaned across his desk and lit it. Oliver turned it in the flame. He had never done that before and decided he must have learned how from the movies. He recounted all the objective details of the story, ending with his arrival that morning in the publisher's office. Then he added, "How *is* Mr. Mather, sir?"

"We don't know. We don't even know why he's in the hospital. Chief Vollhaus said only that he was acting strangely. But General Counsel will find out."

"What's going to happen to him if he doesn't come back to the magazine, sir?"

"I'll worry about that."

"Don't you think I ought to know, sir?"

"Are you trying to impress me with your concern for your colleagues?"

An unexpected and unwanted whine came into Oliver's voice. "It's just that people will be asking me, sir, and if I don't tell them they'll think I'm holding out, sir."

"So, hold out! They'll also want you to tell them what your new salary is. Will you tell them?"

"No, sir."

"How much are you making now?"

"Three hundred and twenty-one a week."

"How would five hundred suit you?"

"Very well, sir." They paused, then Oliver said, "What's going to happen to Mr. Arf?"

The publisher smiled and buzzed his secretary. "Memo to Personnel: Oliver Bacon is now in charge of Quiff. Assistant editor will remain open for a while. Stop interviewing for Plants Aplenty. Memo to Auditing: Oliver Bacon to publisher's payroll at twenty-six thousand, with proportionate stock options. Tell Promotion to get up a release on Bacon for Wednesday morning's papers!" He clicked off the intercom.

"Arf, sir?"

"What would you do with him? I gather from what you've told me this fiasco was his idea."

"I'd keep him. He's a good man."

"You might have an enemy there. At any rate, let's go down to Quiff. I'll make the announcement. You get together a few words to say afterward." He signaled his secretary. "Call Mather's girl and have her collect the staff in the editor's office! I'm coming down to see them." He turned to Oliver. "You said something about more humor in Quiff."

Oliver raised his eyebrows.

"Let them wait a few minutes. It does the help good."

"Maybe we should talk about the help, sir."

The publisher nodded; and, instead of a few minutes, they spent twenty, Oliver describing the strengths and weaknesses of the staff. At the end, the publisher said, "You know, Oliver, I've never felt so close to Quiff. My father started the magazine fourteen years ago on the advice of an assistant. It was a time when girlie magazines were coming up. I was doing a stint in the advertising department and I thought it was beneath the company. In some ways I still do. But it's made money and it's stayed out of trouble—till now. I've really had no complaints about Mather—till now. He's an odd fellow, although he's always been dedicated, in his way. He's not married, is he?"

"No, sir."

"Was he ever?"

"Not that I know of, sir."

"Well, maybe it's time we put him out to pasture. There's an opening on Plants Aplenty."

"Is that a pun, sir? Out to pasture, Plants Aplenty?"

"It is, isn't it? Well, Oliver, let's go down and face the music." The publisher stood up.

Oliver was thrilled at being addressed by his first name. He wondered whether he should reciprocate. If the publisher's first name hadn't been Oswald, he might have. As it was, he merely said, "Yes, sir," and stood up himself.

Oliver had ridden in the elevator beside the publisher perhaps twenty times; but he had never been *with* him, sharing the deference, respect, watchful smiles, and general good feeling that came from all the people getting on and off. Suddenly Oliver was wholeheartedly glad he was getting the job. No more struggling with intermediaries. Now he would be directly responsible to the true boss. And, while fashioning phrases for his little inauguration speech, he vowed one thing: he would be the same kind of boss to the people under him that the publisher had been to him this morning. Forthright, strong, decisive, fair. Sentences formed in his mind. "This will be a shop in which each of us can fulfill himself, not only in his professional capacity, but as a person." "Freud himself said that the two important ingredients of life are work and love—in that order." "I don't want you to think of this as *my* office but as an extension of *your* office, the part where you and I meet and decide how to put out a better magazine." As they approached Quiff's floor his heart swelled with gratitude at the gratitude he felt the staff would feel toward him.

The Quiff offices were divided into two parts: a large, barnlike space cluttered with filing cabinets, bookcases, typewriters, and steel desks; and the editor's office, a four-windowed, carpeted, bepictured, mahogany and glass room with private bath. Over the years he had spent at Quiff, it had seemed to Oliver that Mather had systematically made the staff's working place busier and uglier, while adding touches of parlorlike elegance to his own office. It helped emphasize the difference between the staff and the boss.

The gathering in the editor's office resembled the New Year's Eve party Mather ordered every December 31—

which also happened to be his birthday, so that everyone sang "Happy Birthday" to him. Now, though, people were gathered into tight knots, and the room was full of nervous cigarette smoke. The knots loosened as Oliver and the publisher walked in. Cigarettes were extinguished, those sitting rose, ties were straightened, dresses smoothed.

The publisher began talking immediately, giving the impression, it seemed to Oliver, that his time was more valuable than that of all the others together. "Ladies and gentlemen, let's get right to the point. You now have a new editor. You all know Oliver Bacon and if you share my opinion of him you all like and respect him. Mr. Mather will be taking up other important duties in the company, which will be announced shortly. Let me give you a moment to absorb that." The publisher, however, paused only a second. "Let me say right off that I think you've done a good job on Quiff. As I was telling Mr. Bacon, Quiff was started by my father when he was publisher, and at the time I didn't think it was a good idea. It has turned out to be a very good idea indeed. The world has caught up with the idea, and Quiff is now one of our most important publications. I won't tell you how I think Quiff can be improved, because I honestly don't know. If I did, I might take over the job myself—since I imagine some aspects of your work here must be very interesting." He stopped for laughter, which two members of the staff provided. "I don't think Quiff can be improved because I think there's anything *wrong* with Quiff. I think Quiff can be improved because I think all our magazines can be improved. A magazine is like a person, not perfectible but improvable. Now it's going to be Oliver Bacon's job, with your help, to make a better magazine of Quiff. He and I have talked, and I want you to know I like his ideas. I'll leave the details to him. Now, if any of you have worked on other magazines in the company, you may have heard me say this before. It's not original with me. I heard my father say it many times, starting many years ago. It's this: A magazine must change with the times. Now Quiff is a monthly. . . ." The publisher paused with an instant of uncertainty at this statement. When there were no demurrers, he went on, ". . . and it must change *monthly*. But in a certain direction. It must not circle back on itself, repeating the January or February issue of the year before, even if the fact is that readers don't remember that far back. It must change *in a straight line,* and that straight line must *reach into the future.* It is not enough for a magazine to reflect what's going on now. That's a newspaper's job. A magazine must tell me what's going to happen *tomorrow*. In some cases it may even *make* what's going to happen tomorrow happen. So what I'm asking you is not only that you don't put out *last* year's magazine, but that you don't put out *this* year's magazine. I'm asking you to put out *next* year's magazine. With that said, are there any questions, any questions at all?"

The copyboy said, "Who do we see for raises?" Everyone laughed.

"That, I'm glad to say, is now in Mr. Bacon's province. Anyone else?"

Someone moved in a far corner, and Mather was revealed, smiling mechanically, hunched over as if his large head were too heavy to hold up. The publisher responded without a change of tone. "And what do *you* have to say to all this, Ernest?"

The staff parted. Mather coughed in a quasi-manly way and put one hand into his pants pocket. "Oswald, all I can say is that everything, but everything you have said reflects my thinking *exactly*. I never heard you say these things to another staff, because, frankly, I've spent all my time with you on Quiff. So the words are new to me, but not the ideas. Perhaps I learned them from your father. But they are part of my thinking now. Next year's magazine is *exactly* what I've always tried to put out. Still, Quiff *can* be improved. I believe it. There is no *doubt* about it. A magazine *is* like a person, improvable, except, perhaps, unlike a person, perfectible too. None of us claims to have attained that perfection—I least of all—but we've tried, tried very, very hard. I might also say that these years on Quiff have been good years, very good years indeed. Nonetheless, I look forward to my other duties very, very much. In conclusion let me merely add, 'The king is dead, long live the king.' "

There were a few seconds of silence after this speech. The publisher nodded his head bouncingly through them, then looked up, raised his hand like a master of ceremonies, smiled, and said, "And, Oliver, you must want to tell us something."

"No, sir, not really."

"Nothing?"

"No, sir."

The publisher stared at Oliver, and Oliver shook his head.

"Then let's be about a bigger and better Quiff," the publisher said with closing finality and moved through the people to put an arm on Mather and guide him from the editor's office.

Everyone immediately clustered around Oliver. They all remained fairly quiet until Mather and the publisher were out of the way. Then they took both of Oliver's hands, squeezed his shoulders and arms, rubbed and patted his back. The stenographer kissed him, and someone mussed his hair.

"Let me through!" the copyboy said and put an imaginary microphone in front of Oliver's face. "Mr. Bacon, would you like to make a statement about your new job?"

"Yes, I think it is a wonderful opportunity."

"To do what, Mr. Bacon?"

"Make more money."

"For the company, Mr. Bacon?"

"For me."

"Do you intend to share it with your underlings, sir?"

"Not if it means less for me."

"Then you see this as essentially a one-man opportunity, Mr. Bacon."

"Not so far as work is concerned. I promise to dedicate myself to get each and every man to work himself to a frazzle."

"And won't such work be rewarded, Mr. Bacon?"

"Only if word of it leaks out of the office."

"You want us to be anonymous drones, is that it, sir?"

"Not entirely. I believe in putting blame where blame belongs. In fact, I believe in putting blame where it doesn't belong. In short, I intend to carry on in the manner of my predecessor."

"Here, here!" someone said, and two editors picked Oliver up by the legs. "For he's a jolly good asshole, for he's a jolly good asshole, which nobody can deny."

They carried Oliver in a sitting position into the outer office. There at the far end stood Mather and the publisher watching. Oliver struggled down onto his feet. The song died. The publisher took Mather's arm and led him from the offices altogether. Some of the staff looked apologetically at Oliver. "It's OK, kids. It can't hurt that I'm held in awe by my colleagues. Don't worry! Kids, I have a lunch date"—which wasn't true.

"One hour for lunch, Mr. Bacon," the copyboy said.

Once on the street Oliver wished he had someone to phone. He could step into a booth and ring Long Island, but what would the news mean to her? Just that he was making more money. She might even get the idea that he was now ready to take her away from Gus. Brooklyn would want to come over in the evening with a bottle of booze and celebrate. Florida? Better let her be. He would drop a letter to his parents, so they could tell the neighbors that "Oliver has had a very important promotion in New York," but that wasn't the same thing. Arf was really the one to enjoy this with. Well, Arf would learn about it soon enough. No, this was all wrong. The people to enjoy it with were the people most concerned— the staff. He considered them individually. They would now number eleven: four associate editors, the copy editor, a picture-and-cartoon editor, two secretaries, a stenographer-fileclerk, and the copyboy. They were closer to him in this enterprise than anyone. He walked up to the southwest corner of Central Park. All the benches were filled, so he lay on the grass and looked at the blue and white sky for half an hour. It was like being in love.

He got back to the office early. No one was there but Mather's secretary, on the phone. Oliver didn't like her. She was tall, fortyish, and she never seemed to level with anyone. Would he have to keep her? What do you do with old secretaries? She looked up as he came toward her, and he saw in her face the same questions. Of course, he would keep her. She wasn't *his* secretary; she worked for the magazine, just as he did. He would let her know this as soon as she got off the phone. He smiled and winked as he passed her.

The leather of Mather's chair was creased by years of his body on it. Oliver would have preferred his own oak captain's chair. Better not move it in, though. Just sit down and start working. Getting rid of Mather's remains could wait. The desk was carefully decorated with a picture of a middle-aged woman, probably an old photo of Mather's mother; a green blotter in a leather-cornered

holder; a hara-kiri knife, a present from a contributor
who had done a series on Japanese whore houses; a mar-
ble-based pen and pencil set; and a calendar, on which
Oliver found appointments extending two months ahead.
He opened the nine desk drawers one by one. They were
filled with personal and business papers. Oliver couldn't
bring himself to look at them. The whole place had a
rancid air. It seemed as if a nest of spiritual roaches might
lie under the rug ready to hatch. He'd like to have
stripped and fumigated the room and then covered the
walls with white paint.

The secretary walked in. "Mr. Bacon, I stayed through
lunch because there were so many calls. Everyone wants
to congratulate you. I made a list." Most were from people in the building, and most said they would call back.
"And the publisher phoned. He said you should call him
back as soon as possible."

"Would you get him for me, honey."

Oliver looked up. Tears were running down the secretary's face. Oliver jumped to his feet.

"I'm just so happy for you, Mr. Bacon."

"Oh, gee, thanks." Oliver came around the desk and
put a hand under her elbow. At the touch she fell against
him. Oliver could feel her small breasts and one hip
bone. By her forearms he moved her away.

"He was so *terrible*."

"I know."

"No, you don't, Mr. Bacon. I had to be close to him
all the time."

"*I* was his assistant editor."

"*I* was his executive secretary."

"*I.* . . ." Oliver stopped, smiled, and said, "We both have suffered."

"Oh, Mr. Bacon!" The secretary's tears turned to sobs.

"Hey! It's all over now. He's gone."

She released a final sigh.

"And no more Mr. Bacon. I'm Oliver, and you're. . . ." He didn't know her first name. Everyone called her Miss Drinkman.

"Louise," she said, bowing her head and delicately wiping her cheeks with the side of an index finger.

"Louise. Louise, I have a feeling I'm going to need all the help I can get. Maybe this afternoon, if we get a chance, we can have a talk. At this point you probably know more about the job than I do."

"Oliver, did you know he was there?"

"No. Jesus! I thought he was out on Long Island, in a hospital."

"Wasn't it just like him to say, 'The king is dead'? He wasn't a king. No one thought he was a king. Except himself."

"I'll tell you a secret, Louise. He didn't think he was a king either. In his heart of hearts he thought he was a shit. That's why he acted like a shit. Now be a good girl and get me the publisher!"

"Did you know he was there?" the publisher said.

"No, sir. But I thought you handled it very well. It was a difficult moment."

"That was nothing. In my office the poor bastard broke into tears and asked my forgiveness. He said he had put his life in danger to escape from the hospital and get back to his duties."

"Is that true, sir?"

"I doubt it. At any rate, he's agreed to go to Plants Aplenty, and he's keeping his salary, which means he'll be making fifty percent more than the editor."

"He might be happier there."

"Think so? He has a small desk in a dark corner filled with seed catalogues. Also, he'll be working for what my father used to call a ball-bearing lady."

"I always thought she was pretty nice."

"To *plants*. Well, Mather is more vegetable than animal. Maybe he'll get along. He offered to come down and help you for a while. I said I'd ask you."

"I'd rather find my own way, sir."

"OK. But he'll be in to get his things this afternoon."

"I'd like to miss that, sir."

"Not on your life! I want you to see exactly what he takes."

"How can I do that, sir?"

"How? Examine everything. *You* decide what belongs to him and what belongs to the magazine! If he gives you trouble, call me!"

"I guess you're right, sir."

"And something else. Have everyone write a page or two describing his duties!"

"Is that really necesary, sir? Is that a friendly first move with the staff?"

"It's not meant to be friendly."

"Actually I already know what everyone does."

"This isn't for you."

"No?"

"It's for me. I'll look at the memos tomorrow," the publisher said and clicked off.

After sitting at the editor's desk for five minutes, considering how to tell the staff, Oliver decided to ask Louise's advice and called her. No one answered. She was gone, probably to lunch; and there was no one else in the office. Well, it was only five to two. He sat down again and after a number of unsatisfactory attempts composed this memo: "To the Staff: The publisher has asked me to ask you to write a page or two describing your duties on Quiff. Please get it to me before you leave tonight. O. B." He decided to change the signature to "Ollie" and retyped the memo. He was studying the phrasing when the publisher called back.

"Have you told the staff?"

"They're still out to lunch, sir."

There was a pause. Oliver looked at his watch and imagined the publisher was looking at his too.

"Don't say it was my idea!"

"Why not, sir?"

"You figure that out for yourself!" the publisher said and rang off.

Oliver immediately tore his memo in two and dropped the pieces into the wastebasket. Then he retrieved them and tore them into eighths.

At two-thirty, after having taken a call from a reader who wanted to know when Quiff had run its article on a topless shoeshine parlor in San Francisco and another call from Lester Cushman, who congratulated him and kept saying, "It's a small world," he stepped into the outer office. Everyone seemed to be there. He took up a stance at his old desk and called the staff around. Most of them had been drinking. The copyboy looked drunk. But everyone was still smiling.

"Kids, I want you to take time out this afternoon and write me a memo, all of you, on what you do here." The smiles disappeared, except the copyboy's. "Actually I know what you do," Oliver said, "but this is for the record."

"What record?" someone asked.

"The magazine's record. Look, this is important. Just take my word for it and do as I say! Louise, if everyone's not here, see that they learn about it."

"Yes, Oliver."

Heads turned to see why she was suddenly calling him Oliver.

"OK?" Oliver said.

There were a few grunts. Oliver returned to the editor's office and sat down at his desk. He was about to begin going through Mather's drawers when he realized that no one would be doing a memo on his own former assistant editor's job. If the publisher meant to study the memos for a picture of the total amount of work at Quiff, there would be a considerable gap. Oliver decided he would do a memo in the evening at home. There was also a problem of the assistant editor's work itself. He could spread it out among the associate editors, but then each of them might get the idea that he would be appointed to the job. Oliver decided he'd better carry the work himself for a while, to avoid eventual misunderstandings. He was deep in these considerations when he heard a familiar voice at the doorway. "Hello, prick!"

"Arf!" Oliver jumped up and ran around the desk with his arms extended. "You're out!"

Arf walked past Oliver into the room, looking from left to right, ceiling to floor. He touched the leaves of the plants, caressed the back of the visitor's chair, fingered the glass top of the desk, rubbed the toe of his shoe in the nap of the rug. "This is some setup you got here!"

"Oh, come on, Arf!"

"It is." Arf flopped down into the visitor's chair and threw a leg over its arm. "I didn't know you rated so high."

"Come on, Arfie!" Oliver avoided the editor's chair because of its authority and instead pulled a straight-backed chair from the wall. "Tell me what happened! No, wait!" He got up and closed the door. Louise gave him a slightly reproachful look as he did. "So tell me, tell me!"

"You're feeling pretty good there, baby."

"Come *on!*" First tell me how you are! The Old Man asked me what I thought he should do with you, and I said keep him, he's a good man."

"He took your advice."

"Then you're OK."

"Of course, I'm OK."

"You heard about Mother?"

"Of course, I heard about Mother."

"Then you've talked with the Old Man."

"Of course, I've talked with the Old Man."

"Hey, what about telling him I called the police? You know I wouldn't do a thing like that."

"Of course, I know you wouldn't do a thing like that."

"Then why did you say it?"

"Because I wanted you to get the job."

"How do you figure that?"

"He only gave you the job because he thought you wanted it badly enough to call the police."

"I can't believe that."

"You better, baby. Because if he finds out you didn't call the police, you're in trouble."

"Stop it, Arfie! You thought I made the call and you were pissed off. I just want you to know I didn't. And I'll tell you something else. Now that I've got the job, I'm going to do it better than anyone realized it could be done."

"Better than Mother?"

"Than Mother! What did he know about girls, or people—or anything, for that matter?"

"Will you make more money for the company?"

"Yes, and I'll do a lot of other things too."

"Like what?"

"Like we're going to have more humor in Quiff . . . and we're going to get the magazine out of the hands of the creeps and into the hands of reasonable, ordinary people."

"Did you tell the publisher you intend to change the readership?"

"We didn't talk about specifics. We talked about gen-

eral things and we talked about the staff. That's where
the big change is going to come."

"Are you going to can everyone and start over?"

"Of course not. I'm going to see that people here are
treated like human beings. They *are* human beings and
are going to be recognized as such. Out there there are
some very smart, very talented, very sensitive individ-
uals; and I'm going to give them a chance to show their
stuff."

"Do you know what you have?"

"What?"

"A heart-on."

"A *what?*"

"All that semen has backed up and given you a big
heart-on."

Oliver got up, replaced his chair against the wall, and
opened the door to his office. Louise looked up and said,
"More calls, Oliver. I didn't want to disturb you."

"OK, you can put them through now." He went behind the editor's desk and stood there looking at Arf.

Arf didn't move. "You don't mind if I stick around,
do you?"

"Don't you have work to do?"

"I'm doing my work. The publisher asked me to keep
an eye on you. Just ignore me!" Arf said and picked up
an old copy of Quiff.

Louise walked into the office, tentatively because of
Arf's presence. "May I speak to you, Oliver?"

"Speak away! Mr. Arf is observing us for the publisher."

Louise smiled her cautious smile, looked from Arf to

Oliver, then said, "Oliver, I do so many things around here it would take me all night to list them."

Oliver sighed and said, "Just put 'General duties of a personal secretary.' "

"But I'm an *executive* secretary, Oliver."

"OK, 'executive secretary.' "

Louise left satisfied, and Arf said, "Big heart-on."

"If the publisher wants you in my office he'll have to tell me himself. Now you can get out of here."

Arf rose lazily, dropped the magazine onto the seat of the chair, and sauntered out.

Staff members drifted in through the rest of the afternoon with various magazine business and to drop their memos on Oliver's desk. He knew he couldn't concentrate on them and decided to take them home, along with some undone assistant editor's chores, the most pressing of which was heavy editing on an illiterate article called "He Fixed My Piano" by a Texas housewife about her secret twenty-year love affair with a blind piano tuner. So the only thing that now kept Oliver in the office was Mather's visit.

Oliver felt sorry for Mather and while he waited tried to think of something consoling to say to him. The best he could come up with was the need for younger blood, particularly on a magazine like Quiff. This was just what Mather himself would say if the roles were reversed. It therefore might be just the thing, Oliver decided.

At five after six, when the staff was gone, Mather arrived with two cartons and a black porter. Oliver got to his feet and extended his hand; but Mather, staring at the floor, moved behind the desk, pushed Oliver out of the way, and began emptying the drawers.

"The Old Man wants you to take only what's yours," Oliver said.

Mather continued emptying.

"He specifically asked me to decide what was yours and what was the magazine's, but I thought I'd leave that to you, Mother."

Mather went on as if Oliver wasn't there.

"He said I should call him if you gave me trouble, Mother."

Mather started on the second carton.

"Mother, you must realize the need for younger blood, particularly on a magazine like Quiff."

Mather looked up. It seemed to Oliver that his teeth were bared like a dog's. Oliver wondered if the publisher had possibly told him his reconstruction of Saturday afternoon. Suddenly Mather shivered and emitted a wet-sounding fart. Frantically he emptied the last drawer and hurried from the office, waving the porter after him.

Oliver waited two or three minutes, sighed, turned out the light, shut the office door, which was self-locking from the outside, then realized he didn't have a key. Well, Louise had one. She would let him in next morning.

Oliver had meant to get the lock to his apartment changed. The hall light was on, and the phonograph was playing the music from "La Dolce Vita." Who would be listening to that? He remembered using it as background for making love to. . . ? Margie. But that was a long time ago and in his former apartment. Margie didn't have a key to this one.

Florida called from the bathroom, "Oliver, come *in* he-ah and let me *see* you! . . . Oliver, say something, because if it's not you, Ah'm goin' to *lock* the door and *scre-am*."

"It's me," Oliver said, removing his jacket as well as his shirt and undershirt, which were damp in the underarms with the day's nervous sweat.

"Well, come on *in*, like your doormat says!"

"Coming," Oliver said. He put on a clean shirt, kicked off his shoes, and went to the bathroom door. Florida was stretched out in the tub. Her shoulders, midriff, and legs were very tan; her breasts and lower stomach a lighter tan. Her pubic hair had turned blond. "Yes, ah've been sunnin' in the *nude*, Oliver. Don't ask me who *with*! Well, Ah'll tell you—mah everlovin' husband and no one else."

"You look great, honey. Can I fix you a drink or something?"

"Ah don't *drink*, Oliver. You must be thinkin' of all those *other* girls."

"OK, well, I'll get one for myself."

"You come back now! He-ah?"

Although he had planned not to drink until the Quiff work was done, he poured a deep bourbon into a broad glass and settled himself on his bed. The bathroom door was to the far side of the night table. "How have things been going?" he called.

"Oliver, come back he-ah! I didn't *see* you."

"I'm right here. You can see me when you come out."

There was silence in the bathroom for perhaps a minute. Then Oliver heard her get out of the tub and begin drying herself. "Oliver, turn the record over. The other side is the *mean* one."

Oliver did as she asked and returned to the bed. He still felt the energy to do the Quiff work and do it well and he was confident that he would let nothing disperse that energy. As for Florida, he would deal with her as he dealt with door-to-door salesmen: listen without argument to the spiel and then simply say no.

After more alternating sounds and silences, she came out of the bathroom, still naked, and stood by the bedside. "Now I can really *see* you, Oliver. You look un*happy*." When Oliver didn't reply, she said, "You look un*healthy*. Why, Ollie, you look un*strung*."

"Well, I'm none of those things, honey. Let me get you a drink, even if you don't drink. Or sit down! Or something!"

"Ah'm embarrassin' you, aren't Ah, Oliver?"

"No, you're not. But you'll embarrass yourself if you don't stop waving that golden twat around."

"You're a *real* vulgarian, Oliver." Florida sat down on the edge of the bed. Oliver sipped his drink and studied her breasts, as he apparently was intended to. "You ought to get off this, honey, and have some children."

"Would you like me better then?"

She was dropping her drawl, and Oliver decided he would have to wait through this and whatever other phases were forthcoming. "I'd like you then, I like you now, I've always liked you. But I'm not in business any more."

"I can see that."

"I don't think you can."

"You're bankrupt, Oliver, emotionally bankrupt. And everyone is worried about you."

"Everyone who?"

"I and your friends."

"What friends of mine do you know?"

"Well, I *assume* they're worried, because you looked pinched and *crazy*. You look crazy, Oliver."

"All right, now put something on and have a drink, or do *something!* Don't just sit there like a dumb cunt and tell me I'm crazy!"

"Irritability is the first sign."

"Of what?"

"Neurosis."

"Honey, I have a lot of work to do tonight."

"You never brought work home before, Oliver."

"Not when you were here. Anyway, the point is I'm very busy. I'm also tired. I have no time to play games." He swung his feet off the far side of the bed and stood up. He was exhausted.

"That's a symptom too."

"What?"

"Fatigue. It's as plain as can be, Oliver. You're in for serious trouble."

"I'm *not*. Now will you get dressed and beat it! Please, Betty Lou! I have more than I can do doing what I *have* to do." He walked into the living room and sat down on the couch.

In a few seconds she followed, wearing his bathrobe. "Oliver, why do you think I came here?"

"To get laid."

"That's all you know. I came here to help you."

"OK, to get *me* laid."

"I came here because you're in trouble. I know you're in trouble."

"How do you know?"

"Because your doctor told me."

"My *doctor!* I don't have a doctor."

"Dr. Arthur Hoffmannsthal. And don't tell me there is no such person, because after he called I looked him up in the Manhattan directory."

"Oh, baby! He looked himself up in the Manhattan directory. Dr. Arthur Hoffmannsthal is also Arthur Arf, counselor-at-law. Do you remember him?"

Florida put her hand to her mouth. "Is that a friend of yours?"

"Sort of. What did he say?"

"It amounts to the same *thing*, Oliver." Her drawl was coming back. "Your *friend* said you were *sick*."

"Wait till I get a drink! Do you want one now?"

"All right, if it will make you happy, Oliver. But drinking is a symptom too."

Oliver came back with two drinks. "So what did he say?"

"First of all, he said you had been elevated to a very high post. . . ."

"Did he use a German accent?"

"Yes, he did."

"You know who he learned *that* from? Did you answer him with your English accent?"

"And he said the high post was putting you under extra pressure and he said you had become sexually obsessive-reverse."

"Don't you know that no legitimate doctor would call up and interfere in a patient's life like that?"

"He said these were severe measures for a severe disorder. He knew all about our past relationship and he asked me if I was still fond of you. In a nutshell, he thought I should come over here and save you from yourself. And, Oliver, I can tell just from looking at you, he was right, psychiatrist or not."

"You're not drinking your drink."

"Do you know why, Oliver?"

"Because if you drank it you'd lose your discretion and rape me, right?"

"Yes, I'd rape you with my golden twat."

"You get more and more ladylike."

"More and more *woman*like, Oliver."

"Well, wrap up your golden twat and take it home. I mean that, Betty Lou."

"Suppose I won't?"

"I'll leave myself."

Florida thought about this. "On one condition,

Oliver. When you give up this mad idea, you'll come back to me."

"All right, let me think about it. But tonight I work, OK?"

Florida went back into the bedroom and returned in a moment to stand in the doorway naked. "One more look?"

"Very nice. Good-bye."

As Florida dressed, Oliver spread his papers on the coffee table and considered what to do first. The Texas housewife piece had real possibilities, especially the part in which the blind piano tuner teaches her to sing certain notes in response to being touched on certain parts of her body. She would lie face up on the ffoor; and he would kneel beside her, playing melodies as on a piano. Their favorite tune was "The Star-Spangled Banner."

Finally Florida appeared, in a snug white piqué suit. "Oliver, you tell your friend I think you're even sicker than he said."

"You tell him! He's in the Manhattan directory. Arthur Arf."

"I will, Oliver."

When the outside door closed, Oliver went to see that she had really gone. He felt sure Arf would call, and it kept him from working effectively. After a half hour he took the phone off the hook but still couldn't work. After another while he lay back on the couch to take a nap. He dreamed he was sitting in a grammar school class-room. A male teacher, whom he couldn't see, stood in the back and announced that today the class would have a special visitor. At a signal, the monitor rose and brought in a creature of indeterminate sex and age. It was dressed in a wrinkled, floor-length hospital gown; its face was covered with pustules; its eyes were crossed; its hair was patchy and disarrayed. The nearby students leaned away from it. The teacher said, "This is arararara." Oliver couldn't tell whether the teacher had said "a rararara" or "arararara." "What is your arararara?" the teacher asked. The creature didn't answer, although it seemed to know it was being questioned. "Then why do you arararara?" The students mumbled at the creature's failure to answer. "I put it to you, then, that you arararara!" The students in low voices all said, "Yes! Yes!" *"No!"* Oliver shouted and tried to stand up but found that he was stuck in a small chair. He lurched around to face the teacher, but the teacher had moved out of view. Oliver raised his arms. *"It* can't understand, *I* can't understand." "Ah!" the teacher said. "Do you all see?" The children broke into laughter and applauded. Oliver held out his arms in appeal to the creature. It snapped off a mask and removed the gown. Underneath was the school principal in a business suit. Smiling proudly, the principal strode to the back of the room to congratulate the teacher. The school bell rang, making it a perfect lesson.

Oliver woke to the ringing of his downstairs bell. As soon as he could separate the sound from his dream he stumbled to the release button and pushed it. Whoever it was would be welcome. He opened the hall door and walked to the head of the stairs. No one appeared. Perhaps the caller had gone away. But then Oliver heard light, slow steps on the landing below. He walked half-way down the flight. A girl with short blond hair turned the corner. She was carrying a heavy case. Was she an agent for a cosmetics company? He looked at his watch. Ten thirty. Ten thirty in the morning or ten thirty at night? He'd be late for work. No, it was still night.

The girl lifted her face and smiled. "Hi! It's awfully late, isn't it?"

"It's OK. Just so it's not morning. Come up. What's this?" He took the case from the girl and let her pass him on the stairs.

"A projector."

"A protector?"

"A projector."

"I'm half asleep."

"I called, but your phone was busy."

"It's OK. You woke me from a nightmare. What's the projector for?"

"To show you your pictures."

"My pictures?" Was she selling something? Was this sales rhetoric? "Excuse me, but should I know you?"

The girl looked half abashed and half amused.

"Because I don't. I'm sorry."

"Really?"

"I have the feeling you're the daughter of a friend of mine."

"I don't think so, Mr. Bacon."

"Are you from my hometown?"

"Which hometown?"

"You must be a relative of someone, because I *almost* know your face."

"Are you fooling me?"

"No. Tell me your name! . . . Oh, Jesus!"

"You remember me."

"No, but the other day I was asking a Puerto Rican girl, just your size, the same thing. Everything is happening twice in this story."

"What story?"

"Oh, you're Yoyo. With the photographer. What pictures? Did you get them back from the police? I'm sorry. I was asleep or I would have recognized you."

"The police never saw these. Those were Derek's pictures. I just took pictures of you."

"Yoyo! Yoyo! I didn't see you taking pictures. Go in!" Oliver motioned her toward the living room. "I'll be in in a minute." He went to the kitchen, splashed water on his face, and called, "Bourbon OK?"

"I don't drink, thank you," she called back.

"Everything is happening twice."

"What?"

"Nothing. What kind of pictures?"

"At the motel. You'll see."

When Oliver came in with his drink and the projector, she was neatly seated on the couch. Her short hair was curly and shiny, her eyes large, and she had the noncommittal expression he associated with contemporary college girls.

"You looked very cute, in your drawers, holding all those bikinis."

"Were you in jail too?"

"The police chief put the ladies up in his house. You got out before he came, didn't you? Some people thought you called him."

"No."

"I didn't think you did."

"Why did they think that?"

"You were deserting a sinking ship."

"No, I mean, why did they think I would call the police?"

"I don't know."

"Did they say it because I wanted the editor's job?"

"No, I didn't hear that."

"I got the job."

"I know you did."

"How?"

"Mr. Arf told me."

"When?"

"Tonight."

"Tonight!"

"He called me."

"About what?"

"Just to chat."

"Did he send you here?"

"Nobody *sent* me here, Mr. Bacon."

"I'm sorry. Did he *suggest* you come here?"

"When I told him about the pictures, he said I should come here immediately, they might be important."

"Did he say why?"

"I thought you would know. Maybe I shouldn't have come."

"No, no! It's just that Arf is peculiar. I mean, he's been doing peculiar things. It's OK. I'm glad you came. And please call me Oliver. . . . Jesus, there it goes again."

"What?"

"Everything is happening twice."

"You said that before. I don't understand."

"*I* don't understand. Listen, let's look at the pictures."

"Do you really want to see them? I have a feeling I walked in on something."

"You did. But let's see the pictures. Enough talking! How do we show them?"

Yoyo looked around the room. "I'll take the lamp off this table, and you take the paintings off that wall."

"How many are there?"

"Twenty-four. They're darling."

"I'll bet!"

"They are." Yoyo set the projector up on the lamp table and turned out the lights. "You tell me when I should change them!"

The initial pictures, showing the half-clad models smiling up at Oliver with stagey seductiveness, were amusing. Then the pictures became repetitious: Oliver alone, stiff and tall, lips thin, eyes looking nowhere. He stopped her and studied one.

"What do you see?" she said.

"I see the creature from my nightmare. There was this terribly ugly thing, neither man nor woman, pimply, and cockeyed. It looked *crazy,* like something that had crawled up out of the ocean. That's what I see."

"I see a nice young man who looks ill at ease because of what's going on around him. And that's what you *were.*"

"No. I'm a sadsack, and I'm not just *playing* a sadsack, I *am* a sadsack. Look at me! Just like Mather wasn't *playing* a creep, he *was* a creep."

Yoyo went over and stood beside the image, which was about lifesize. "You see," she said, pointing with her index finger and its shadow, "it has nice curly hair."

"It has a creased and worried brow."

"No. The eyes are intelligent."

"It has pendulous ears."

"You *don't.* They're nice ears, and you have a manly nose."

"Weak chin."

"You have a nice body. It's like a boy's."

"Boney ribs."

"A nice thin waist."

"Wrinkled shorts."

"Athletic legs."

"Knobby knees. Anyway, we skipped something up there."

"What?"

"It doesn't show."

"Oh!"

They were silent for a moment, both staring at the image. Then Yoyo turned the projector off and the room lights on. "I see a nice person in my pictures, Oliver. I wouldn't have shown them to you if they weren't nice.

You were the only human being out there. Everyone else was making fun of love, and you weren't. That's what I see."

"Sweetie. Yoyo. What kind of a name is that? In the dream, the creature was my boss. The hospital gown, the sexlessness, everything. But it was me too. I'm *becoming* him. Today I even agreed to do his job."

"But you're not like that man at all. You're entirely different. You were *disgusted* by the motel."

"Disgusted? . . . When I came home I wrote an article for the magazine about a man who farts in bed and disgusts his wife. I called it 'Gusts.' I think it had to do with disgust."

"That's what I mean."

"No, I'll show you what I mean. If I asked you to go to bed with me now, what would you say?"

She was silent and showed no expression.

"You'd be disgusted, wouldn't you? . . . Am I frightening you?"

"No. But I really just came over here to show you the pictures."

"Let me put it another way. I'm not asking you to go to bed with me. But, if I did, what would you say?"

She thought for a while. "I'd say I don't know you well enough. I don't think I'd enjoy it, and I don't think you would either. Would you enjoy it?"

"I'm about to say yes. But I don't know. No, of course I'd enjoy it. But I'm not asking. It's just that I've had to think about screwing for, I don't know, weeks. And now I look at you and I don't have to think about it any more.

That sounds funny. I mean I've been *meditating* on screwing and now I don't have to meditate."

"That sounds like you're really asking me," she said and smiled.

"No. Here's what I mean. If I screwed you. . . ."

"Made love to me."

"If I made love to you, I wouldn't have any qualms about it."

"Do you have qualms about making love?"

"Yes."

"Why?"

"Sweetie, I don't *know*. . . . I'm crying."

"I can see that."

"Everything is happening twice."

"I wish you wouldn't say that."

"I can't help it. It *is*."

Yoyo held out her hand. He looked at it.

"I'm holding out my hand."

"I can see that," he said.

Yoyo laughed. "That just happened twice."

"Yes, everything," he said and took her hand. "May I say something?"

She nodded.

"The touch of your hand is like the touch of genitals when you're making love to someone you love. . . . Does that upset you?"

"I think that's very nice."

"I'm going to take my hand away," he said, "it's starting to sweat."

They sat silently for a while, looking at one another. Oliver occasionally sucked in his lips and clicked his tongue. Finally he said, "What are you going to do?"

"What do you mean?"

"What are you going to do now?"

"I have to go home."

"You're not married or anything?"

"I'm not *married*."

"You're living with someone?"

"In a way."

"With Derek?"

"In a way."

"Look, will you do something very important?"

She nodded.

"Will you please not make love with him tonight?"

She was silent.

"Promise me that you won't make love with that shit tonight?"

"I wasn't planning to, and Derek's not a shit."

"No, I didn't mean that. I don't know Derek. But you won't, will you?"

"No."

He sighed. "Where will you be tomorrow?"

"When tomorrow?"

"All day."

"I'll be out on a story in the morning, and in the studio in the afternoon."

"Derek's studio?"

She nodded.

"OK. Will you call me in the office in the morning?"

"Oliver, you're out of breath."

"I know. Am I making a fool of myself?"

"No."

"When will you call in the morning?"

"When do you want me to?"

"Ten?"

"OK."

"I'm really not acting like a fool?"

"No, Oliver."

They exchanged numbers and went down to the street. He put her into a cab, bounded up the stairs, and immediately went to bed to think. Instead he fell asleep and dreamed he was standing on a tile path that stretched far away. On both sides of the path were high tile walls. At the far end the tiles were bright orange and yellow, but the closer they were to him the dirtier they seemed. Outside the walls were the events of his life. They had made the tiles dirty. He could not see the events; but they were there, each in its chronological place. If he concentrated, he could discover what the events were; but they didn't seem important. The important thing was that they had dirtied the walls. The tiles were so beautiful at the far end! At the far end he had been born. At the far end a girl appeared and ran toward him. As she passed the tiles, they turned bright orange and yellow. The girl ran fast, but it took a long time for her to reach him. She fell into his arms. He could feel every part of her body against him. Over her shoulder he saw that all the tiles were an equally bright orange and yellow. Even in his dream he knew this was the best dream he had ever had.

Louise, the copyboy, and three staff members were already in the office when Oliver arrived on Tuesday. He bid each good morning, and each returned the greeting. On his desk was the mail, open, preread and neatly piled; beside it a Times, a Daily News, and a Wall Street Journal. The previous day's papers had been removed. The only other object on the desk—Mather had taken even the blotter—was a new marmalade jar of sharpened pencils. In the top right-hand drawer was a fresh supply of letterhead bond, large and small; corresponding envelopes; plain bond; and copy paper. There was a delicacy about the quantities that made Oliver think of portions in a good restaurant. The carpet had apparently been vacuumed overnight; the nap lay one way. He walked to the four windows. In the thousands of times he had been in this office he had never observed the view. Why was that? You had to keep your eye on Mother. Now by bending close to the far window and looking through two rows of office buildings he could see the Hudson River. He poked a finger into the plant pots; the soil was nicely damp.

Louise hissed from the doorway, "The publisher!" She barely had time to get out of the way.

"Good morning!" Oliver said cheerily.

"Do you have the memos?"

"Yes, *sir!*" Oliver swept up the envelope in which he had brought them to and from his apartment and dumped the contents onto his desk. He separated the memos from the manuscript of "He Fixed My Piano" and handed them to the publisher. "Sit down, sir! I'll go on doing what I'm doing. You'll find, by the way, that my old job isn't described there. I was going to write it up. . . ." The publisher had begun reading.

Oliver wondered what he should do while the publisher read. If he were still the assistant editor, he would have sent for coffee and leafed through the Times (a copy he would have bought in the lobby), then with more care looked over the local stories in the News. The Wall Street Journal he attended only when it ran a pertinent feature —on chemical aphrodisiacs, say, or sex symbolism in car design, or American youth giving up underwear. So normally it would have been the Times, the News, and the Journal, in that order. Now, not to impress the publisher but simply because he was the editor, he started with the News; and, sure enough, on page four was a piece about a mass rape in Riverdale that gave him an idea for a symposium. Ask convicted rapists whether rape had been their only sexual outlet. Had they had regular girlfriends? Did they feel affection for their victims after the act? He made a note to himself.

The publisher removed his glasses. "Have you read these?"

"Actually I took them home, sir. . . ."

"Who is N. B.?"

"Ned Breakstone, sir. Very good man, as I told you."

"Yes, well let me quote N. B. 'Arrive promptly 9:30,

when (1) have gotten to bed the night before, (2) alarm goes off, (3) wife makes breakfast (sometimes she makes Breakstone), (4) trains run. Shave in men's room. Back at desk by ten. Comb old copies of Playboy for new Quiff ideas. Visit Medical to ogle receptionist, who doesn't know I exist. Back at desk, console self with latest Sex, Pleasure, Kiss, Screw. . . ."

"He was just gagging around, sir. He thought the memo was for me."

"I understand that. B. D. writes: 'In spring I sow, in summer tend, in autumn reap, in winter enjoy.' "

"That sounds like William Blake, sir."

"Who is L. S.?"

"The copyboy, sir."

"L. S. says that the atmosphere at Quiff has led him to resume his adolescent habit of masturbation. He asks that a hole be drilled in the bottom of his desk drawer so he can keep both hands free for filing."

Oliver giggled. Louise came into the office and excused herself to the publisher. "Oliver, there's a lady on the phone. She says you expressly told her to call at ten. It's very important."

"Put her on! I'll just be a minute, sir." Oliver picked up his phone. "Yoyo, you remembered! . . . Yes, me too. I had a beautiful dream about you. . . . You *did!* . . . Come have lunch with me! I can see New Jersey from my window. . . . Then dinner! . . . Five thirty, sixth floor. Hold on!"

The publisher had dropped the memos on Oliver's desk and walked out.

"That was the publisher. . . . Of the whole company.

Hey, listen, he had me get the staff to write up what they do here. Fortunately—because, boy, were they gagging around!—he's a perfectly regular guy. Let me read you one. Here! 'Monday: invent contributors to take to a week of imaginary expense-account lunches. Tuesday: collect leftover artwork to sell to Sixth Avenue porno shops. Wednesday: line up Quiff models for publisher and his wife. Thursday: line up remaining models for myself. Friday: rest up for wild weekend.' "

Louise came into the office, laid a note on Oliver's desk, and made a face to indicate its importance. Oliver nodded, and Louise left. He went on talking to Yoyo for twenty minutes. After making her promise to call back at eleven, which by then was twenty-five minutes off, he hung up and read the note. "The publisher wants you to call him as soon as you're off the phone and have finished the comics."

Oliver smiled and shouted out to Louise, "OK, honey, get him!"

Louise reported that the publisher had left his office.

"He'll call back if it's important. So what do you think of the universe?"

Louise smiled cautiously.

"Come on, it's better than that. Sit down, and we'll answer these beautiful letters from our beautiful readers."

At eleven Yoyo didn't call. Three minutes later the publisher called. "What issue are you working on?"

"February, sir."

"How often does the staff meet?"

"Well, sir, Mr. Mather met once a week. . . ."

"When is the next meeting?"

"I. . . ."

"Have it this afternoon!"

"This after. . . ."

"At two thirty. I want to watch," the publisher said and clicked off.

After sitting still for a while, Oliver opened the desk drawers, one by one. Except for new supplies, they were empty. He went out to the copy editor and asked if he had the February schedule. He didn't. Oliver asked Louise. No. Did she have the schedule of articles received-and-read, received-and-back-for-revision, commissioned-and-unreceived? Not a recent one. Mr. Mather must have it.

"Get him!" Oliver said and went into his office to wait for the call.

Mather wouldn't be in to his new job till the afternoon.

"Get him at home!"

No one answered there.

"Get the publisher!"

The publisher had left for an early lunch.

While Oliver was wondering what to do, Yoyo called and explained that she had been unable to get to a phone at eleven. He told her about the problem of the forthcoming meeting and the missing schedules. "I can fake it. But that's not what I want to do. I have a feeling that Quiff is better off without all that tired old material. Even the things I've been dreaming up myself have that creepy brown tinge to them. Maybe this is the time for Quiff to strike out in a new direction."

"What direction, Oliver?"

"I don't know. I just have the feeling."

They both were silent for a while, then Oliver said, "Do you read Quiff?"

"Derek has it around."

"What do you think of it? Be honest!"

"It's the same old thing every month."

"Right! The same old thing month after month. If we're going to put out not *last* year's magazine, not *this* year's magazine, but *next* year's magazine, we've got to break with the past; and that means breaking with schedules and plans. It means getting rid of Mother once and for all. . . . Tell me something! Given the fact that it's the same old thing, what's *wrong* with the same old thing?"

"Well, Oliver, you can imagine how a female feels about a magazine like Quiff."

"You mean, women are treated like hunks of meat."

"No, it's that all the girls always look the same."

"Wait till I get a pencil!"

"I'm not going to say anything important, Oliver."

"We'll see. Go on!"

"I don't think Quiff girls are the girls men are most interested in."

"Go on!"

"My theory is that men are much more interested in ordinary girls."

"What kind of ordinary girls?"

"*Very* ordinary girls. Look at it this way. Most men get married, right?"

"OK."

"And most men marry the girl they love, right?"

"Yes."

"And most girls are ordinary, so most men must really love, or be interested in, ordinary girls. . . . Oliver, are you there?"

"I'm thinking. . . . Yoyo, you're a fucking genius. . . . I'm sorry. You're a genius. Really, you just invented the Quiff of the future."

"Have I, Oliver?"

"You have come up with the one idea that has eluded every girlie magazine editor in the country. In the world! . . . Listen, sweetie, call me! No, I'll call you. Or, if I don't, I'll see you here at five thirty. I have"—he looked at his watch—"two hours to fill this idea out. Good-bye! Say good-bye!" She said good-bye. "Louise, come in here and bring your beautiful, beautiful pad!"

For an hour Oliver talked, and Louise wrote. Every now and then she made a low swooning sound. "You like that?" Oliver would say. "Oh, Oliver!" she'd answer, twitch her bottom, and turn a page. When he was done, he said, "Can you stay through lunch and type that up?"

"Oh, yes, Oliver. And, Oliver, may I say something?"

"Sure."

She leaned over and kissed him on the cheek, then hurried out to her desk. Her typewriter went at great speed for an hour. While he waited, he refined some of the arguments, discarded some, and thought up some new ones.

At two o'clock, Louise brought in her work—twelve pages, with two sets of carbons. "It's full of errors, Oliver. I didn't think I should take the time to proof it."

"Small errors," he said, "but one large truth."

"Oh, yes, Oliver. Yes, yes, yes!"

At two thirty Oliver went into the outer office, stood by his old desk, and announced that the publisher would be down at any minute for a meeting with the staff in his office. Would everyone please come in. Oliver took Mather's old seat at the head of the conference table. All the associate editors had put their jackets on, and everyone sat up with a certain formality. There wasn't an empty chair. Oliver said, "I think this may be a very important meeting."

After a silence, the picture-and-cartoon editor asked what it would be about.

"A new Quiff," Oliver said, "a really new Quiff."

"In what way, Oliver?"

"Well, I don't want to shoot my bolt before the Old Man arrives, but let's say I think it's just what he wanted when he asked that we put out the magazine of the future."

"Give us a hint, Mr. Bacon!" the copyboy said.

"Let me first say that the publisher as yet knows nothing about this. It will be as new to him as it is to you. He may not buy it at all."

"The way you're smiling, Ollie, he'll buy it."

"Frankly, I think you'll all buy it. But while we're waiting, let me put a question to you. When a man falls in love, what is it he falls in love with?" Oliver beamed at them, turning his face around the table like a searchlight. Someone hiccoughed; and the publisher walked in, followed by Arf.

Everyone rose. Five people stepped away from their chairs. The publisher took one, Arf another. Two editors were displaced; they stationed themselves against a wall. Everyone else sat down. The publisher nodded at Oliver. He cleared his throat. "I was just asking the staff, sir, what it is that a man falls in love with when he falls in love with a woman."

Silence.

"All right, let me put it another way. Does a man fall in love with a woman's exterior or her interior?"

Arf barked. The copyboy giggled.

"Does a man fall in love with what a woman appears to be or with what she is?"

"Mr. Bacon," the publisher said, "are we discussing the February issue?"

"Yes, sir, we are. We're discussing the entire future of Quiff. I won't beat around the bush. . . ."

Arf barked again.

"I maintain that men, men generally and men readers of Quiff, are not *essentially* interested in the fare we've been serving them. I think they're interested in *real women.*"

"We've been serving them falsies?" Arf asked.

"Yes! We've been serving them *womenlike* creatures.

Month after month, year after year, the same big-busted, thin-waisted, plump-rumped, dead-eyed falsies. . . ."

"What do you suggest we serve them?" the publisher said.

"Real women, sir."

"What kind of real women?"

"*Very* real women."

"I don't follow you," the publisher said.

"Well, sir, have we ever published a picture of a flat-chested woman—even though there are millions of flat-chested women in America, whom American men, *our* readers, have fallen in love with and married? Have we ever published a picture of a woman with overly large thighs? With a thick waist? With stubby fingers? . . ."

"With a bald spot, one eye, hairy tits, two assholes?" Arf said.

"I'd like to see the last one," the copyboy said.

"You're missing my point," Oliver said. "I don't suggest we go scavenging Coney Island for grotesques. The woman must have a *quality* . . . a quality that makes her capable of being *loved*. We could touch men much more deeply by showing the *womanness* of women. Look at it this way! We come out with a four-color fold-down of, let's call it a *plain* woman. The reader is shocked. This is not what he has come to expect from Quiff. So what does he do? He asks himself why Quiff has done this. They must be telling me something. And what is that? It's that here is a woman like the woman I fell in love with and married. Here is a woman I could really care about. Here is a woman, not that I want to *screw,* but that I want to *live* with." Oliver paused for a response, but everyone merely stared at him. He went on: "We have a February Whiff of Quiff, a March Whiff of Quiff, an April Whiff of Quiff. They're all the same. What men want to look at is a *unique* woman."

"Which one is that?" Arf said.

"July," the copyboy said.

"Are you suggesting that we show these 'real' women clothed or unclothed?" the publisher asked.

"Nude, of course, sir," Oliver said. "I claim that men will find them more beautiful than models."

"Ollie, my boy," Arf said, "there are plenty of cheapie one-shots in the porno shops filled with the kind of dogs you're talking about. They'd only make Quiff look like it couldn't afford better."

"That's a point," one of the associate editors said.

"All right, let me go on, because what I have in mind reaches beyond cheesecake. I'd also like to see an article by a well-known swordsman who's man enough to admit that he never enjoyed sex so much as with the girl he really loved, no matter what she looked like. I'll go further and suggest that we run an article arguing for temporary abstinence. . . ."

"You can call it 'Abstinence Makes the Heart Grow Fonder,'" Arf said.

"Good title," Oliver said. "I also suggest we run a geri by an old man who has been faithful through fifty years of marriage and is proud of it."

"I have an idea," Arf said, "a pixshtick about a guy who decides to give up sex. We see him, one shot after another, turning away from luscious, naked babes, the kind with the big tits and small waists, until finally he's all alone. What happens? His head begins to swell up. Then his arms and legs. He gets as big as a Macy's balloon. And he bursts. We do it with lens trickery."

"I also suggest," Oliver continued, "that we commission a poem. . . ."

The publisher stood up. "Oliver, thank you. I must go. Come see me when the meeting's over. You too, Arf," he said and left.

Oliver, who in his argument had stood up, sat down. "Commission for each issue one poem about love. . . ."

" 'There once was a man from Nantucket. . . .' " Arf said.

"Arf, why don't you trot along. I'd like to discuss some internal matters with the staff."

"OK, Oliver," Arf said, getting up, "but I want you to know something. I want you to know that you're an amateur. In fact, you're a *professional* amateur."

After Arf left, Oliver leaned wearily over the conference table. "Does anyone want to comment on these ideas?"

One of the associate editors suggested that such changes ought to be made slowly. One such picture and article in the February issue; then test the response. Someone else claimed that single examples surrounded by the old type of material would be taken ironically. Louise said she thought the publisher hadn't given Oliver a chance to explain his ideas completely. Everyone agreed with that. Someone suggested that if the changes were adopted the magazine might be called Quife, a play on Quiff and wife. Someone said that if a department on booze were added the magazine could be called Quiff and Quaff. Oliver broke in. "I better go and see what the verdict is. For all we know, we may just put out the February issue as planned." Everyone agreed that that was a good idea.

Arf was sitting in the publisher's waiting room. Oliver took a seat as far from him as he could, but Arf came over and sat next to him. "You're not angry, are you, baby?"

"Why didn't you back me up?"

"I want to keep *my* job."

"Are you saying I don't want to keep mine?"

"Do you? . . . I had lunch with your friend Betty Lou today."

"You deserve one another."

"She has a body like a cello. How is she in bed? What does she like?"

"Everything."

"She's still sweet on you, baby."

"Why did you send Yoyo to my place?"

"I thought she might put you out of your misery. Was I right?"

"Maybe."

The publisher's door opened, and Mather came out with the publisher's arm around him. Mather's big head was held high, and he seemed full of new inner strength.

After bidding the publisher good-bye and thanking him
—one could tell, for the fifth or sixth time—he strode toward the elevators, looking neither left nor right. "Oliver,
come in! You don't mind, Arf—we won't be long." As
soon as Oliver got within reach, the publisher put the
arm around him and guided him into the office.

"I'll get right to the point, Oliver. Your ideas are use-
less for Quiff. If we were somehow selling a man's magazine to women you'd make a brilliant editor."

"I'm fired."

"Not at all. You have real insights, not into men, but
into women's ideal of men. In fact, I'm surprised you've
stayed on Quiff so long. It makes me realize even more
keenly that Mather has been the guiding spirit down
there. He showed me his February schedule; and, I must
say, it's not at all bad."

"It's the same old thing."

"Of course. Surely you know the one ironclad rule of
magazine publishing: never publish a feature that has
not previously been published in another magazine. And,
if a magazine has been around as long as Quiff, the rule
becomes: never publish a feature you haven't previously
published yourself. Gardner, one of my assistants, expressed an even nicer refinement: never publish anything
that does not appear elsewhere in the same issue."

"What about what you said to the staff?"

"Oliver, you wouldn't make a statesman either."

"I'm fired, then."

"No, no. You're a nice young man, and I'd like to put

you where your, shall we say, domestic impulses can take root."

"You mean Plants Aplenty?"

"Exactly."

"I don't know anything about botany."

"Neither did Mather, but he was willing to learn. And you said you liked the editor."

"You said she was ball-bearing."

"That doesn't matter in an office, Oliver."

"And Mather?"

"I want him to have another crack at Quiff. He's had a bad shaking up, but I think he still has something to contribute to Quiff. Well, what do you say?"

"A desk in a dark corner with the seed catalogues?"

"We can do something about that."

"I suppose I'd keep my salary, the way Mather did?"

"That's about what the editor herself makes."

"If I promise to try to get her job?"

"Well, all right. . . . So you've come out pretty well, Oliver."

"I have, Oswald, and I'll tell you why. What you want to buy from me, for five hundred dollars a week, is a warm body pressed against a steel desk. You also want a head that has learned to make its way and take its place in a hierarchy that you sit on top of. Yesterday I sirred you for over an hour. It was like the key note; every time you heard it it must have been music to your ears. But, you know, right now I don't feel any dumber than you, any uglier than you, any weaker than you, any sadder than you. And I'll tell you something else. You're going to die before me. What kind of surrogate daddy will you have been then? I won't even be asked to the funeral. I'd have become an old middle-aged man and I'd have never grown up. But if I walk out of here, I'll be an adult and your equal. You'll go home to your townhouse, and I'll go home to my apartment. Will you take a bath with purer water than I will? Tomorrow morning we'll both eat a nickel egg. When we walk in Central Park will you breathe sweeter air? Will you see greener grass? . . . I was going to say, will you fuck a prettier girl than I will? In fact, let me ask you a question: have you slept with the most beautiful girl you have ever seen? Answer me! I've already quit."

The publisher considered the question. "I can't say I have, Oliver."

"Well, there you are, Oswald."

"I suppose I could have if I had pressed the matter. . . ."

"Anyway."

"Yes, anyway. Oliver, you have unexpected balls. My father used to say of Winston Churchill—he knew Churchill quite well—that he had unexpected balls. . . . I believe my father slept with the most beautiful girl he ever saw. He said to me once, when I was grown, of course . . . but that's another story. Oliver, come back and see me in a month or two and we can talk."

"You mean, in case Mather doesn't work out?"

"No, perhaps you'd like to try something new for me."

"A man's magazine for women?"

"Perhaps."

"Stick it up . . . Mother's ass, Oswald!"

"You're not playing the game, Oliver."

"That's right," Oliver said, turned, and walked out of the office. As he passed Arf he called out, "Next!"

Oliver stood outside looking into the Quiff offices. The staff was gathered around his old desk. The serious talk had apparently ended. One editor was showing the label of his tie to another. The copyboy had his hands tucked into his armpits and was flapping his elbows in rendition of some beast or person. Louise clutched a handkerchief in her skinny fingers but was nodding pleasantly at whatever the picture-and-cartoon editor was saying. The scene reminded Oliver of those unexpected gifts of time in grade school when the teacher had suddenly been called from the classroom. He really shouldn't break it up. He should go down to the lobby for a cup of coffee. No, maybe it was just that he wanted to remain editor in their heads a little longer.

Louise saw him, made a motion, and everyone turned, like birds in a flock. They spread in an arc to receive him, and although he approached smiling, he could tell from their faces that his face gave the news away. The arc closed around him. "Children, I'm no longer editor of Quiff, or assistant editor either. Mother is coming back." Someone said it had all been too good to be true, someone else said that he knew he should have asked for that raise before lunchtime. Generally the mood derived from

Oliver's mood, which was not so low as he thought it would be. A collection was made, and the copyboy went out for scotch; so that by five thirty, when Yoyo arrived, no one was feeling any pain, or at least not much.

Yoyo among these intimates added a pleasant tension. She really is a pretty, pretty girl, Oliver thought, so sweet in her candy-striped dress, younger than anyone present, brighter, happier, more expectant of the good things in life. Except for her large, wise eyes and little come-and-go smile, she might have been a teen-ager. Oliver meticulously introduced her to everyone. She already knew the copyboy from East Hampton, and they made jokes about the adventure. No one told her the news.

As soon as Yoyo and Oliver could break away, she said, "You promised to show me your office."

"Yoyo. . . ."

"Can you really see New Jersey?"

"Come on!" He let her go in. She walked around slowly, looking at this and that like a bride in a new apartment.

"Don't say anything about the office, will you?"

"Why?"

"I'll tell you at dinner."

"Where are we going?"

"Someplace nice."

"To celebrate?"

"Yes. Then I'll take you to a make-out movie."

She said nothing.

"Then I'm going to take you home and make love to you all night long."

Yoyo looked over her shoulder to see that no one could hear, paused, and said, "Oliver, there's something I must tell you."

"What?"

"I shouldn't tell you."

"What, what?"

"I'm a Teresean."

"A *what?*"

"I'm a member of the Order of Saint Teresa."

"A *nun?*"

"I've been sent out secretly into the world to influence magazines like Quiff."

"*Influence magazines like Quiff!*"

"Purify them."

"Yoyo, I've fallen in love with you."

"I know, Oliver, and I'm sorry."

"Oh, my God! . . . We can have dinner, can't we?"

"Of course."

They went to La Côte Basque and afterward saw a revival of "A Man and a Woman." In the next three months Oliver was glad he had no job because it took three months of constant argument to convince Yoyo that she could serve God married to him. The quality of their marriage is not known, as is the case with most of the recent unions of religious and laymen.